"Will you..."

There they were, the words Emily had waited half her life to hear.

She had imagined it a hundred times or more.

Sitting on the banks of Willow Kiss, she had dreamed of Matthew kneeling beside her, taking her hand and asking her gently, earnestly, to be his wife...forever.

She had never, however, imagined herself sitting on an olive-green bedspread in a budget motel while Matthew implored her to "be practical" and marry him.

"Why do you want to do this, Matthew?" she asked softly. "You've explained why you think we should get married, but you haven't explained why you want a child."

"A kid should know who his father is. I want to be there. I want to be involved in the child's life."

"And this marriage," she asked hesitantly, "would it be permanent?"

"No one can answer that question, Emily."

Dear Reader,

This month, wedding bells ring for six couples who marry for convenient reasons—and discover love by surprise. Join us for their HASTY WEDDINGS.

Kasey Michaels starts off the month with *Timely Matrimony*, a love story with a time-travel twist. It's all in the timing for modern-day bride Suzi Harper, and Harry Wilde, her handsome husband from the nineteenth century. Just as they found happiness, it seemed Harry's destiny was to leave her....

In Anne Peters's *McCullough's Bride*, handsome rancher Nick McCullough rescues single mom Beth Coleman the only way he knows how—he marries her! Now Nick is the one in danger—of losing his heart to a woman who could never return his love.

Popular Desire author Cathie Linz weaves a *One of a Kind Marriage*. In this fast-paced romp, Jenny Benjamin and Rafe Murphy start as enemies, then become man and wife. Marriage may have solved their problems, but can love cure their differences?

The impromptu nuptials continue with *Oh, Baby!*, Lauryn Chandler's humorous look at a single woman who is determined to have a child—and lands herself a husband in the bargain. It's a green card marriage for Kelsey Shepherd and Frankie Falco in *Temporary Groom*. Jayne Addison continues her Falco Family series with this story of short-term commitment—and unending attraction! The laughter continues with Carolyn Zane's *Wife in Name Only*—a tale of marriage—under false pretenses.

I hope you enjoy our HASTY WEDDINGS. In the coming months, look for more books by your favorite authors.

Happy reading,

Anne Canadeo
Senior Editor

Please address questions and book requests to:
Silhouette Reader Service
U.S.: 3010 Walden Ave., P.O. Box 1325, Buffalo, NY 14269
Canadian: P.O. Box 609, Fort Erie, Ont. L2A 5X3

OH, BABY!

Lauryn Chandler

Silhouette
ROMANCE™
Published by Silhouette Books
America's Publisher of Contemporary Romance

For Matthew Bradley Warren—
a unique and wonderful brother,
a unique and wonderful man.

 SILHOUETTE BOOKS

ISBN 0-373-19033-6

OH, BABY!

Copyright © 1994 by Wendy Warren

This edition published by arrangement with Harlequin Enterprises B. V.

® and TM are trademarks of Harlequin Enterprises B. V., used under license. Trademarks indicated with ® are registered in the United States Patent and Trademark Office, the Canadian Trade Marks Office and in other countries.

Printed in U.S.A.

LAURYN CHANDLER

has wanted to be an actress since she was seven. Her parents suggested that she establish a secure career to "fall back on," so she decided to become a novelist, too. She finished her first book when she was fourteen—a very long short story about a San Fernando Valley hockey team and their dying goalie, who happened to be a woman. "I figured I could play the lead when the book was made into a movie," she remembers. After graduating from U. C. Irvine, she became a waitress with dreams of glory. One day, she wrote another book, sent it to Silhouette and, as she puts it, "Here I am, doing what I love!"

June 19, 1972

Dear Diary,
Guess what? I went to
the creek to spy
on boys. There was
a boy there named
Matthew Carter ♡♡♡?
He is very VERY cute!
I fell in the creek
when I was spying on him
and he pulled me
out.

(Why am I so embarrassing
???)

He walked me home! I
hope we will be friends.
Love xxo
Emily Carter
(JUST kidding)

Prologue

May, 1984

Matthew Bradley Carter, I'll love you till the day I die.

Emily Isabel Gardiner paused on the threshold of a white runner that traveled across green lawn and led to an altar one hundred feet away. From where she was standing, she could see the minister, two bridesmaids, the groom's men ... and Matthew.

Her fingers tightened around the handle of her rose-and-gardenia bouquet. For just a moment, she closed her eyes. She would never forget this day ... how perfect it all was. The scent of the rose petals ... the feel of the sun ... the rustle of taffeta ...

Emily heard the bar of music that was her cue to walk up the aisle, and her eyes snapped open. She looked toward the altar, where Matthew stood grinning. Her knees started shaking.

How did brides do it? she wondered. How did they walk toward their grooms without melting into little silk-and-lace puddles right there in the aisle?

Taking her first, trembling step, she focused on his smile.

He was the handsomest groom she had ever seen ... the handsomest groom in the world! His eyes were blue; his hair was gold; his face was tan. He looked like the sun and the sky and the earth, and the feelings he aroused in her were just as elemental.

When she reached the altar, Matthew winked. It was only the single, slow blink of an eye, meant to encourage because he saw that she was nervous and meant to tease for the same reason. A wink wasn't much, but it made Emily's pulse thud heavily in her throat.

Oh, Matthew, she promised again silently, and as solemnly as a child swearing a blood oath to her very best friend, *I'll never stop loving you.*

She stood there, gazing at him, memorizing him, just a moment too long.

The crowd behind her began to shift. They stood.

Matthew's gaze lifted an instant before the music changed and Emily was jolted into awareness.

Embarrassed to have slowed down her part in the proceedings, she turned and moved to the left as swiftly as she was able. She walked with the odd step-hitch-step gait she'd had since she was a child, but no one among the wedding guests took any notice. Most of them had known Emily all of her twenty-two years. Only she was aware of her own imperfection, and she felt it keenly as she turned to face the aisle, as the strains of the Wedding March filled the spring air, and as her cousin Jessica glided along the pristine white runner with all the poise and all the loveliness that were a bride's inherent right.

She looks like a princess, Emily thought, *going to meet her prince.* Not a soul present would have thought that notion too fanciful.

They were a golden couple, Matthew and Jessica, the pride of True, Oregon. Two young, beautiful people, made for each other, united by desire—both their own and the desire of others to see them together. Looking at them gave the very old a fleeting chance to feel young again, ready to taste the world. It gave the still young something to dream about.

It gave Emily both of those feelings. But, moreover, looking at them now gave her a deep and abiding sense of guilt. She had grown up with them, played with them, fought with them. She loved them both.

Jessica was her cousin.

Matthew, her best friend.

Surely it was wrong to feel envy. It was wrong to be anything less than happy today, of all days. But try as she might, she could not keep herself from imagining...from wishing...from longing. She could not keep the ache in her heart from filling her eyes and her throat when the bride and groom joined hands.

And as the vows were being spoken, Emily Gardiner could not escape the feeling that as her cousin's life was just beginning, somehow the best part of her own life was coming to an end.

Chapter One

"Pass those peas and pearl onions, would you, Emily dear?"

Tillie Gardiner held out two delicately veined hands and smiled gladly as she received the bowl of vegetables from her great-niece. The elderly woman's hands trembled as she set the bowl on the cloth-covered table and reached eagerly for the large serving spoon. "Oooh, mmm-mmm, pearl onions," she fairly squealed in anticipation. "I love pearl onions."

"Shouldn't eat them. Gives you gas." Lillian Gardiner, Tillie's twin sister, grumbled from across the table. She heaped a mound of mashed potatoes onto her own plate.

Emily suppressed a smile as Tillie's mouth compressed into a skinny, wrinkle-rimmed line. The twins—as the spinster sisters had been referred to now for three generations—were at it again.

"Pearl onions do not give me gas, Lilly Gardiner." Tillie's prim, ladylike voice pinned her sister like an arrow. "And I'll thank you to mind your own biscuits."

"I share a room with you, Tillie Gardiner," Lil shot back, her own voice as deep and crackling as Tillie's was high and tinkling. "It most certainly *is* my business."

"Aunties!" Emily broke in as lightly as she could without sacrificing effectiveness. She resisted the urge to clap her hands to gain the women's attention as they bristled at each other, relying instead on a diversionary tactic.

"Do you know who came into the library today?"

Emily tucked a lock of long red hair behind her ear, picked up her fork and toyed with a piece of pot roast while she waited for one of the aunties to respond. Refusing to continue a story until they asked for details was the best way she knew to gain their interest.

Fraternal twins, the women differed as greatly in appearance as they did in manner. Tillie was small and plump and feminine. Lil was flat as a plank and twice as straight.

Tillie eyed Lilly, gauging her willingness to switch subjects. Lil complied by asking, "Who?"

Emily smiled. In the years since they had retired as co-librarians of the True Public Library, neither aunt had relinquished the notion that the library was her own personal property—her home, in fact. Eight years ago, at the age of twenty-four, Emily had stepped into the position her aunts had vacated.

There had been Gardiner women at the library's helm for forty-nine years now, a True, Oregon, tradition that made Emily a little proud and a little sad.

Sad, because it was always a *single* Gardiner woman who ran the old library, cataloging the books and watching over the people who checked them out the way a homemaker cares for her house and her family.

That life had been acceptable to her aunts, but for Emily the fit was growing increasingly uncomfortable. For the past couple of years, she had been thinking more and more about the future that stretched before her. And recently she had come up with a plan, one that was guaranteed to bust wide open the tradition set by her forebears.

All she had to do now was muster and maintain the courage to go through with it. It would help if she could talk it over with someone, get some support. But who in the town of True would understand what she was about to do? Most of the people she had grown up around made Ozzie and Harriet look like radicals. Her mother and father would be shocked—no, *appalled*—when they found out, and her aunts . . .

Emily shook her head very slightly, a small smile touching her lips. Her aunts would fall face-first into the whipped potatoes if she made her announcement now.

"Why are you smiling? Who came into the library?"

Lil's voice recaptured Emily's attention. Slipping her cat, Jo, a bite of pot roast, Emily answered her aunt. "Newl Higgins came in today. Right before lunch."

"Newl Higgins!" Tillie dropped her fork, uncharacteristically allowing it to clatter onto the china dinner plate. She clasped her ivory hands over her thin bosom. "Oh, Emily, you didn't let him use the rest room, I hope. The last time he used our rest room, he tried to flush bubble gum down the urinal.''

''That was a long time ago, Aunt Tillie. Newl is in his fifties now.''

''Newl Higgins does not respect books!'' Lil sided with her sister. ''He hasn't stepped foot in our library since 1952, and that was to put a garter snake in the girls' lavatory...''

The sisters discussed Newl's various offenses until Lil announced, ''I have more interesting news than anything about Newl Higgins. No offense, Emily dear.''

''None taken, Auntie.''

''I saw your aunt Ginny in Hurwertzer's Grocery today—he's overcharging on bulk grains again, wouldn't you know it—and do you know what she told me?''

''What?''

''Matthew Carter is home. He's staying at his uncle Fisher's old house. Fisher willed it to Matthew several years ago, may he rest in peace.''

''May he rest in peace,'' Tillie mumbled dutifully. ''Oh, I'm so glad somebody's finally come to fix up that old place. It's looked so lonely all these years. How long will Matthew be staying?''

Emily sat very, very still. She said nothing. No words could have come up past the sudden tightness in her throat and no pot roast could have gone down. *Matthew Carter is back in True.*

It had been five years since they had seen him last, a brief ''How-are-you-we're-so-sorry'' conversation at his mother's funeral. He'd been living in Boston for years, and he and Jessica had rarely made it back to their hometown. They had brought their parents east for visits. Jessica hadn't even returned for her mother-in-law's funeral.

"I hope he stays for Memorial Day," Tillie continued. "The picnics are such fun." She shook her head sadly. "He's had a difficult life for a young man."

Lil ran a gnarled finger up the moisture on her ice-tea glass and nodded. "Mmm-mm. First his mother going like she did. She was a good woman, may she rest in peace."

"May she rest in peace," Tillie echoed again.

Lil sighed roughly. "And then—" She stopped, folding her hands beneath her chin. "I've lived over three-quarters of a century—three-quarters, mind you—and I still find it hard to believe that so much sorrow could come to one family. Especially to such a nice young man. Always so polite and considerate." She shook her head. "And so respectful of books. It was a pleasure to have him in our library."

"Yes, it was," Tillie agreed, her small, faded blue eyes twinkling, "just a pleasure. Oh, I do hope he'll stay for Memorial Day. Do you remember when he and Emily won the sack race?" She clapped her dainty hands. "That was so exciting! When was that?" Tillie frowned. "Was it the spring we changed the lighting over the nonfiction section?"

"No, no." Lil reached for a bowl of pickled beets. "It was the year the roof leaked over reference."

"I don't think so. Emily, how long ago was that? How old were you when you and Matthew ran in the sack race?"

Emily's gaze lifted to her aunts.

"Fifteen," she murmured. "I was fifteen."

Memorial Day, seven years ago. The day Matthew Carter had convinced her to enter the holiday-picnic sack race.

The day he had shown a girl who had only ever limped what it felt like to run.

It seemed like a lifetime ago.

It seemed like yesterday....

"Matthew Carter, I am not your personal property, and I will run in the sack race with anyone I please! Besides, Danny Clark asked me *hours* ago, when *you* were too busy to be bothered."

Jessica tilted her pretty nose in the air and swung away with a swirl of blond hair. Matthew stared after her with his hands on his hips and his jaw clenched.

From her spot under the maple tree, Emily heard and saw the entire conversation. She would have felt like she was eavesdropping, if not for the fact that Jessica had deliberately spoken loudly enough for several people to hear her rejection of Matthew's invitation to be his partner in the couples race. Now Jessica was going to be stuck inside a burlap sack with Danny Clark from the race's start to its finish and she wanted Matthew to stew over it. And all because she was angry at Matthew for working on the chair he was carving instead of picking her up early for the picnic.

Emily frowned. Dating was a complicated venture. She knew so little about it. She never would have chosen Danny over Matthew—she certainly wouldn't have talked to Matthew like that in front of so many people—but Jessica probably knew more about dating than anyone in town, and she and Matthew always made up after a fight.

And Matthew didn't look too upset. He turned, caught Emily watching him and sauntered toward her. Emily blushed to the roots of her red hair.

The horrible truth was that she was glad Jessica fought in public and made up in public and teased in public. She was glad for any opportunity to see into their relationship.

She was probably a voyeur. She should probably talk to the school counselor about it, or to Reverend Soames. What if "Thou shalt not spy" had become a commandment recently?

Matthew dropped to the grass beside her. He hooked an arm over one bent knee and smiled at her crookedly. "Guess I'm in the doghouse with your cousin again."

Emily smiled back and tried madly to tamp down the blush that threatened to wash through her again.

She'd been blushing an awful lot lately. She'd known Matthew since she was ten years old. They were best friends. But lately she felt so...*aware* around him. Not aware of *him*, actually, as much as she was aware of herself.

He swayed toward her, knocking her shoulder with his arm. "So, whaddaya say, Emily Mo Cremily?"

Emily looked away from him and shrugged. He'd been rhyming her name for as long as she could remember. And for as long as she could remember, she had liked it.

"Hey, Matt!" It was Peter Bloom, walking toward the picnic grounds with his arm around Hillary Mason. "You gotta find a partner and register for the race, man." He squeezed Hillary's shoulders. "We want to beat your butt."

"Next year." Matthew grinned, waving them on.

They watched Peter and Hillary walk away, and Emily ventured, "I'm sorry you won't get to be in the race."

"What's the prize this year?"

"A watermelon."

Matthew leaned back against the tree and laughed. "Oh, well." He picked up a dry twig, kept his elbow on his knee and rolled the twig between his teeth. "I like this time of year. Trees are green, the wood's not too dry yet."

Emily studied the progress of an ant hiking through the blades of grass and said nothing. Already, at seventeen, Matthew looked more like a man than a boy. He looked, she thought, like Robert Redford.

They sat quietly for several minutes, watching people trail off in couples to register for the sack race and watching the breeze ruffle the leaves. Then Matthew turned his head and looked at Emily through narrowed blue eyes.

"You want to be my partner in the sack race, Em?"

She felt as shocked as if he'd asked if she wanted to fly to Rome by flapping her arms. Matthew laughed at her expression and asked her again.

"Come on, Emily, I bet we could win. You've never entered any contests as long as I've known you."

"You know why I haven't."

For years, Matthew and Matthew alone had encouraged her to push beyond the limits scoliosis had inflicted on her. He'd pushed her all over town and back the year she was confined to a wheelchair after an operation to straighten the curvature of her spine. She had barely been out of the wheelchair when he'd insisted on teaching her how to float on her back in the water. That was the year *The Poseidon Adventure* had come out. Matthew had seen the movie eleven times and then insisted that if she ever went on a cruise and the ship capsized, she would need to know how to float.

He had never, however, up until today, tried to talk her into making a fool of herself in front of the whole town.

"Now, why do you look like that?" Matthew swiveled around to face her.

Unfurling the scowl that had claimed her features, Emily had no qualms about expressing her anger in a furious whisper. "You know I can't run in a sack race or any other race. If you're just trying to prove a point with Jessica, I don't appreciate your using me to do it!"

"Em. Em!" Matthew reached for her arm when she started to get up. He held on and squeezed gently to get her to look at him. "When have I ever needed to prove a point with Jessica? She likes a lot of attention. She always comes around eventually. And when have I ever taken advantage of our friendship?"

Emily tried to shrug the question away, but Matthew held fast. "When, Em? I was just sitting here, watching everybody else walk to the race, and I realized I've never asked you before if you wanted to enter one."

He sounded slightly embarrassed, and when she finally turned her head to face him, she thought he looked disgusted—but with himself, not her.

"I'm not your responsibility," she told him quietly, feeling warm and grateful and frustrated and hurt by the idea that he might, indeed, consider her a responsibility.

His hand dropped from her arm to her fingers, and he pressed them gently.

"You're my friend, Em, that's all I meant. At the moment, you're a very touchy friend." His teasing tone made her smile just a bit, and he pressed the advantage. "Do you trust me?"

With my life, she could have said the moment she looked into his honest blue eyes, but the angle of his cheeks, the strength of his jaw, the curve of the lips that seemed to look more masculine every day, held her as silent as the dandelions that waited for a breeze to blow them into motion.

The dandelions were lucky. There wasn't a force strong enough on the planet to make fifteen-year-old Emily take action. She trusted Matthew, but she could not bring herself to tell him that her feelings for him were growing... and changing. Nothing would make her risk rejection from the one person who could make her feel whole and accepted and could even make her forget at times that she was bound by restrictions most people her age knew nothing about.

"I guess I trust you. A little." She shrugged, her tone as teasing and light as if Jessica had said the words.

Matthew grinned and stood up. He held out his hand.

"Let's go, then."

"Where? I'm not entering a sack race, Matthew."

He crouched in front of her again. "Just tell me one thing, and be honest. Would you do it if you thought you could win?"

"I don't know. I mean, they're only giving away a watermelon." She looked at the smile in his eyes. "I suppose I would. But only if I *knew* I would win." She protested as he grabbed both her hands and pulled her to her feet. "Matthew—"

He held up one shushing finger. "I promise you'll win. Come on."

The watermelon aside, she had been victorious, indeed, Emily recalled now with as much affection and outright gratitude as she had felt for Matthew that day. To know what it was like to participate, to feel as young and free and *fleet* as any other teenager—that was the victory Matthew had given her.

And here, sitting at her dining table, entertaining her aunts for the evening, she felt a twinge of the buoyancy she had felt when Matthew propelled them both across the finish line ahead of every other couple in the race.

"However did you win that race, Emily?" Tillie asked merrily. "Every other team fell and fell, and you two never lost your footing!"

A dimple peeked from Emily's cheek. She had stood on Matthew's feet, holding on to the sack while he wrapped his arms around her waist.

"It's a secret. Matthew made me promise never to tell a living soul."

"We're seventy-four. We barely qualify as living souls anymore." Lil's mouth twisted.

Emily leaned back in her chair, opting to rub Jo's head, rather than finish her dinner. "Oh, Aunt Lilly, you're sharp as a tack and live as a wire, and you know it."

"That's right, and so am I!" Tillie glared at her sister. "Now, Lil and I will make a little something— tuna casserole and a nice gelatin mold would do well,

I think—and you can take it over to Matthew in the morning, dear."

"Me?" Emily squeaked, straightening in her chair. "Oh, Aunt Tillie, I don't think so. We lost touch years ago after he and Jessica moved to Boston. I wouldn't feel right just barging in on him now. And he'll probably be so busy seeing people—"

"Oh, don't talk nonsense, Emily! His father and the people he grew up with are the only family he's got left. The more company the better, in this case. It's been over a year since Jessica died. We need to help him reestablish his roots."

"And he has to eat," Lil pitched in. "Shame you two lost touch." She clucked her tongue. "Hard to keep up with all the changes life brings. But he certainly was a nice young man. Just like his uncle Fisher. Polite and helpful and very smart. You don't become a lawyer with mush for brains, not in this day and age." She nodded approvingly.

Emily reached for her ice-tea glass. A nice young man. A good man. An intelligent man. Yes, indeed. And, she would have added, a man with humor and sensitivity.

Just exactly the kind of man I need.

She paused with her hand halfway to her glass.

Was she crazy to even think it?

Matthew was alone now. As alone as she was—or more so, because he knew what it was like to have a mate and to lose one. Surely he would understand her desire to create a family of her own. To have someone to give her whole heart and life to. To have a child.

For years, Emily had believed that somewhere, someday, she would meet the man with whom she could build a home. She hadn't been expecting Mr.

Right or a knight in shining armor. Just someone nice, someone good who wanted to share a life. And she had a fine imagination—she could have filled in whatever blanks there were.

But the good man hadn't come, and the one time she had gone out looking for him had been a disaster too great to think of often.

She had gone on a cruise. A *singles'* cruise.

An awful cruise.

The Voyage of the Damned.

The Poseidon Adventure in slow motion.

She hadn't told anybody the real purpose of the cruise, and she never would. But she had come to a decision at the end of it: She was through waiting. She was going to begin her life. By herself. She was going to have a child.

She had researched every option as thoroughly as a librarian knew how, and she had come up with her answer: artificial insemination. She had contacted a clinic in Portland and received additional information from them. The scoliosis might make pregnancy a bit more difficult than it normally had to be, but it would not prevent her from carrying a baby.

The only gnawing concern she had was not knowing who the father of her child would be, but now . . .

If she renewed their friendship and told him what she planned to do, then at the very least—the *very* least—she would have a friend who would understand and support her decision. And if she asked him and he said yes . . . Well, then she would ask for nothing more from this lifetime.

A sweet smile crossed her face at the thought of holding her own child in her arms—a child fathered by Matthew Carter.

"All he can do is say no."

Emily realized that she had whispered the encouragement out loud when Tillie laughed.

"Well, of course he's not going to say no. Who ever said no to one of my gelatin molds?"

"Maybe I'll make blueberry corn muffins. Muffins are man's food," Lil declared with all of the assurance of a spinster who was sure she knew what men liked.

"You'll take everything over to him tomorrow morning then, Emily dear?"

Emily looked at her twin aunts, single all their lives and childless, and wondered how different their lives might have been if they'd had the option to become single mothers when they were her age. She wondered what her life would be like when she was their age if she didn't take advantage of that option now.

She nodded slowly. "Yes, I'll take everything over tomorrow."

Chapter Two

Matthew leaned over the wood he'd been working on since shortly after sunrise.

The saw he held felt good in his hands. The rhythmic motion of his laboring body felt good, too.

For too many years his only exercise had been the socially correct type: occasional jogs and frequent trips to the gym. With the exception of lifting an unusually heavy brief or a volume of Massachusetts state law, life as a corporate lawyer in Boston did not require manual labor. He hadn't had a callus in years. Now his hands ached and his shoulders ached and his back hurt. It felt great.

He drew the manual saw back, his elbow arching high before he pushed the blade forcefully through the wood. The grind of metal teeth against oak almost masked the ring coming from the direction of the house.

Matthew stopped sawing and listened. The door-bell.

"Damn it." He glanced up and noted with disgust that he'd left the back door open. The bell pealed again, carrying clearly across the yard.

"Go away," he muttered darkly, returning to his wood.

He'd been back in True two days now. He hadn't contacted anybody to tell them he was returning—not Jessica's parents, not his own father. No one.

But that hadn't stopped the True, Oregon, grape-vine from wrapping him in its stranglehold.

Somebody must have seen him open the house, be-cause they had come in waves yesterday afternoon: first his mother-in-law and then her friends, all the town biddies bringing him casseroles in exchange for a little gossip about the local boy made good, the suc-cessful city lawyer and the reason for his sudden re-turn.

Well, it was none of their damned business. Noth-ing he did was any of their business anymore.

When he had left True with Jessica on his arm and an acceptance to Harvard Law School in his pocket, he'd been everybody's hero, the local golden boy, and he had known it. He had known it not in the manner of a young man whose conceit overwhelmed his good sense, but in the manner of a man who had carried the burden of other people's expectations and other peo-ple's dreams until he hadn't been certain any longer where *their* needs ended and *his* needs began.

And so the gossips had come to see how the lonely widower was faring. And to bring him their casse-roles. And to tell him about their granddaughters and their nieces—lovely girls, so bright and attractive, and a couple of them still single, imagine that.

The mere sight of him had caused a few of the women to stumble in their rambling reports, and the thought of it brought a grin to Matthew's face now.

They might have forgiven him his appearance, he knew, if his attitude had been better. But he had lost the art of civil babble. Or rather, he had lost the patience for it.

The doorbell pealed one last time and then, blissfully, was silent.

Matthew continued sawing, feeling the knot in his gut relax a little as the possibility of a solitary day stretched before him. He was just beginning to enjoy himself again when a voice interrupted his work.

"Matthew?"

Without looking up, he lifted the saw from the wood and slammed it to rest on its side. Resting his palms on the plank, he hung his head in defeat. "Damn it."

It was only ten o'clock in the morning, with a cool breeze, but Emily felt perspiration trickling between her shoulder blades as though it were high noon. She was nervous almost to the point of being sick.

She'd stood on Matthew's porch for a full five minutes, her arms laden with food, her heart laden with trepidation as she waited for him to come to the door. Finally, she had followed a dim sound around to the backyard.

She had seen immediately that there was someone in the large backyard shed, but she wasn't at all certain that someone was Matthew Carter. The man in the shed was considerably leaner than Matthew had ever been. His hair was long and straggly, and from what she could tell in the outbuilding's shadows, he was sporting a moustache and beard.

Also, either he was hard of hearing or not in the mood for company, because he showed no inclination to turn around.

"Matthew?" she said again tentatively.

Grudgingly, the man straightened up from the plank of wood he was leaning on, turned around slowly, as though the motion took more effort than he had in him today and walked into the light of the yard.

Only his eyes were exactly the same, just as blue as she remembered.

Matthew wore jeans and a pair of very old cowboy boots, and that was all. No shirt, no belt and no welcoming smile.

Emily tightened her hold on the gelatin mold and hitched the tuna casserole up higher onto her good hip.

"Hi." Her voice sounded nervous and breathy. "It's me. Emily."

Matthew didn't bat an eye. His expression—or lack thereof—never changed. She wasn't even certain that his lips moved when he said, "Hello, Emily."

"I heard you were in town." She attempted a smile. "I brought you a few things. Some food. In case you get hungry."

He nodded. Once. And she thought he sighed. "You'd better come into the kitchen, then."

He kept his eyes on her face until he walked past her to lead the way through the back door. In the kitchen, he made no move to take the dishes from her hands. He went directly to one of the cupboards, opened it and surveyed the contents, standing with his back to her.

"You drink coffee?"

"Sometimes." Distracted by his demeanor, Emily answered as though the question were general rather than specific.

He looked at her over his shoulder. "Now?"

"Oh. I would drink it now, yes."

He nodded, pulled two mugs from the cabinet and walked to the stove. "You can put those dishes on the table."

His voice was still smooth and deep. That, along with his eyes, was familiar. She set the dishes and a box of chocolate-glazed doughnuts—his favorite kind and her own contribution—on the kitchen table and sank onto one of the ladder-back chairs.

Why had she thought last night that this would be easy? Alone in her house, she had considered asking Matthew to help her, and the more she had thought about it, the more plausible the idea had seemed. She would renew their friendship and eventually work the conversation around to her plan to have a child.

Maturity, openness and good humor—she had half convinced herself that was all she would need to introduce the topic of artificial insemination into the morning's reacquaintanceship.

So, how've you been?

Fine. You?

Oh, fine. Looking for a sperm donor.

Emily shook her head. How utterly ridiculous the idea seemed now. Her heart sank. She hadn't even spoken to him in years, and by the look of him he'd be content to let a few more years pass.

She would leave. She would drink her coffee, exchange a pleasantry or two and then exit more gracefully than she had come in. But she would not—she

could not—discuss something so intimate with someone she hardly knew anymore.

"Cream and sugar?" Matthew's voice barely dented
her thoughts.

Overwhelmed by a feeling of defeat, Emily heard
him as if he spoke from very far away. She nodded
miserably at the table and sighed. "I'd love sperm."

A moment passed.

Her head came up. Her eyes opened wide.

"Some!" The emphatic correction was practically
a shout in the silent room. "I'd love *some*...some...if
you have it. Or if not, then just coffee will be fine...."

Her voice dwindled away pathetically. She whipped
her gaze from Matthew's and prayed fervently that he
had somehow missed her first mumbled words.

His face remained impassive as he set the mug of
coffee in front of her and went to the refrigerator for
milk. He pulled a box of sugar from the cabinet, a
spoon from a drawer, and put everything onto the table. Seating himself in the chair across from her, he
picked up his own mug.

For several long moments he sipped his coffee in silence. Emily could feel him watching her. When he finally spoke, she jumped.

"You've changed, Emily." His tone was lazy and
matter-of-fact, with no implied judgment or praise.

"Have I?" Plastering a bright, too gay smile on her
face, she busied herself with cream and sugar.

"Mmm-hmm." Matthew hooked an ankle over a
knee and leaned back in his chair. "I didn't know you
even knew the word *sperm.*"

Emily coughed and sputtered as the sip of coffee she
had just taken nearly choked her.

Matthew laughed. His chest shook, his head fell back like he was enjoying a good breeze, and he laughed and laughed in a way that changed not only his expression but apparently his mood, as well. The darkness that hovered around him seemed finally, briefly at least, to lift.

When he was able to, he put his coffee on the table, leaned forward over his elbow and asked, "What made you say that?"

Emily looked at the broad white smile she remembered so well and found that she was torn between feeling a little bit better and feeling much, much worse. He was right—she didn't think she'd ever actually said the word aloud before. And at the moment, she was convinced she would never, ever utter it again.

She reached for the purse she'd deposited on the floor by her chair. "My mind was on something else."

"Obviously."

"No, I didn't mean— Oh, never mind what I meant."

Angry at herself for babbling like an uncomfortable fool, and angry at him for making her feel uncomfortable from the moment she'd walked up to the shed, she stood to leave.

"Heat the tuna casserole in a three-hundred-and-fifty-degree oven when you want it and refrigerate the gelatin mold."

She nodded sharply and started to walk past him. Matthew remained in his chair, but snaked a hand out to grab her before she slipped by.

"What about the doughnuts?" He nodded toward the table. "You remembered that I like chocolate."

The laughter subsided, but the warmth in his eyes remained.

"I'm sorry, Em. If you'll stay a little while, I promise to be more civilized."

Em. Her name never sounded as good as when Matthew said it. She sat back down with her purse in her lap.

"Emily Gardiner." Matthew lifted his coffee cup, but paused before touching it to his lips. He raised a brow. "It *is* still Gardiner, isn't it?"

"Yes."

He took a sip of coffee and nodded. "I thought so. I hadn't heard anything to the contrary, but then I haven't kept up with all the latest gossip."

"You don't stay in touch with Aunt Ginny?"

Matthew stiffened immediately at the mention of his former mother-in-law. He made no reply. Emily didn't really need one. Aunt Ginny had lamented on many an occasion that Matthew rarely wrote or phoned.

There seemed to be nothing else to say for the moment.

Sitting across from him today was so different from sitting next to him on the bank of Willow Kiss all those years ago. Back then their conversation had flowed as freely as the water in the creek.

"When I get older, I'm going to build furniture. I'm going to have my own store, and I'll build everything in it."

Even at the age of thirteen, Matthew had known what he wanted. And so had eleven-year-old Emily.

"I'm going to be a wife. And live right here on the creek and have lots and lots of babies."

She almost sighed aloud at the memory. So many plans. But life had wound up leading them, rather than the other way around. Matthew's parents had balked at the notion of their son as a carpenter. Well, practicing corporate law in Boston was a long way off from building furniture in Oregon. And holding guardianship over a lot of books was a far cry from having a family. Did he ever miss not having his furniture store? she wondered.

"I'm sorry I wasn't able—"

"Listen, Emily, I apologize for not—"

They had both broken their silence at the same time, and they each gestured for the other to go ahead.

Matthew shook his head. "Ladies first."

Emily warmed her hands on the mug. "I was just going to say that I'm sorry I couldn't make it to Jessica's funeral."

He nodded slowly. "Massachusetts is a long way away. I was going to say that I'm sorry I never returned your call. I appreciated it, though. And the note."

Again they were quiet, but this time there was a burgeoning return of warmth, of comfort in the silence, an echo of what they'd had in the old days.

"So, tell me about your life, Em. I know I'm a heel for not staying in touch, but catch me up now."

More than ever, Emily wished she had done something unexpected, if only once. What could she share other than that she'd done what they had all known she would do: she had followed in her aunts' footsteps and become the trusty—if lonely—librarian.

She ran her finger over a chip in the table top. "Well, I—"

Matthew was watching her with a look of patient interest on his face. He'd always been the easiest person in the world for her to talk to, the only person with whom she'd felt really eager to share her secret dreams. Because he'd had secret dreams, too.

"I'm going to build furniture."

"I'm going to have lots and lots of babies."

She had told him her dreams once; why couldn't she do it again?

Emily linked her trembling fingers on the table. She moistened her lips and met his gaze squarely.

"I'm going to have a baby."

Matthew's eyes traveled down her body with such swiftness, she was tempted to laugh. He certainly wasn't going to see anything. Her prim spring dress covered a very slender body and a bosom that wasn't much larger than it had been when they had splashed together in the creek after school.

"I'm not pregnant yet. I'm just—" she gave a stalwart smile "—in the planning stages, you might say."

If Matthew was confused, he chose not to show it.

"I wish you and your friend luck."

"My friend?" Emily's brows knit briefly. "I don't have a friend. I mean—" she could feel herself starting to blush "—I have *friends,* of course. But there isn't a man...per se. I mean, a man I'd want to have a baby with...a father type..."

Damning her nerves, Emily grabbed her coffee and took a hefty swallow. If she wanted help, she was going to have to ask for it, and she would have to ask now, before her courage failed her entirely.

She lifted her gaze from the scarred table. He was still watching her, but she couldn't read his thoughts. The moustache and beard blurred the expression around his mouth.

Lifting her chin, she attempted a clear, strong tone. "I plan to be a single mother. It is my intention to be artificially insemina-a-a—" Choking on the word, she swallowed hard.

In Emily's family no one ever, but *ever*, referred to the human reproductive process—artificial or not—in mixed company. Reminding herself that she was breaking new ground, she cleared her throat and tried again.

"You see, artificial insemina-ation—" her voice cracked, but at least she got through it "—is a respected method of procreation in the nineties. It's really much more common than you might think."

"Uh-huh." Matthew's eyes narrowed. "Let me get this straight. You can't *say* artificial insemination, but you want to do it?"

Emily laughed a little too brightly. "I said it."

He shook his head. "Just barely."

"I can say it," she insisted. "I'm just a little squeamish about certain technical aspects of the procedure, that's all."

"Oh." Matthew's posture was still relaxed, almost lazy in contrast to her stiffness. "What is it that bothers you?"

"Well . . ." Emily straightened her back against the chair and worked thoughtfully through her answer. "For one thing, it disturbs me that I won't know who the father of my baby is. These days they let you go through files to choose the donor. I could pick a doctor or a college student or even another librarian, I guess." She relaxed a bit when Matthew smiled. "But it's not the same as knowing the father of your child— who he is, what he looks like, how he walks—is it?"

"No, I imagine it's not."

Emily nodded. *Courage,* she coached herself. "So, I was thinking about the kind of biological father I'd like for my child, and—" she grinned nervously "—you're probably going to laugh, but I thought, 'You know, Matthew Carter would be a good donor. You could ask him.'"

It became clear immediately that she was wrong about one thing: Matthew was not going to laugh.

He stood up from the table without taking his eyes from her. His expression was much easier to read now. This time even the moustache and beard couldn't hide the grim set to his lips or the tensing of his jaw.

"Are you crazy?" His voice rasped with steely intensity. "Of all the irresponsible, idiotic—" He leaned forward, palms on the table. "I haven't seen you in years. You don't know me anymore. You wander over here with a tuna casserole and a little conversation and you think you can ask me for—" He cut himself off, turning away from her and swearing ferociously.

Emily gaped dumbly in response. She had imagined many reactions, but not this one. Her stomach twisted into knots and she stammered.

"I—I brought a Jell-O mold, too."

Matthew stood at the stove with his back to her. The muscles in his shoulders were tight and tense. When he spoke, his words, too, were taut.

"Go home, Emily."

Miserably, she rose to comply. Clutching her purse, she took a few steps around the table, but before she moved to the door, she felt the need to do something, say something that might possibly make sense of this.

Shaking her head in consternation, she said, "Matthew, I'm sorry. Maybe I could have handled that better, but I don't under—"

He whipped around and only his voice was more thunderous than the look in his eyes. "Emily, go home!"

Chapter Three

It wasn't hard to find Emily's cottage.

Matthew simply looked in the phone book and drove over.

The hard part came after he got there.

All day long his conscience had jabbed him like a needle. He had tried to convince himself that he didn't owe her an explanation, that he hadn't asked for company, didn't want it and had done them both a favor by making himself clear.

Then he would remember the look on her face when he'd yelled at her, and conscience would thwart convenience.

Pressing her doorbell, he listened for the chimes. From inside the house, he heard footsteps, then Emily's voice admonishing, "Back, Jo. Stay back."

When the door swung open, a plump white cat scurried onto the porch. It knocked into Matthew's legs, then scrambled around and leapt onto the wooden railing.

"Jo! Sorry, she—" Emily took a step forward to retrieve her cat, then stopped abruptly when she saw Matthew. Her eyes widened.

Jo hissed.

As silence settled heavily around them, Matthew wondered who was watching him more warily—Emily or the cat. He decided it was Emily. Leaning into the door, she was peering up at him like a child peeping from behind her mother's skirts. She wore the same dress she had worn to his house, but now her feet were bare and her red hair curled loosely about her shoulders. She looked as fresh and young as she had when they were teenagers. For a foolish moment Matthew broke one of his cardinal rules: he allowed himself to regret the passing of time.

He shifted and the porch boards creaked. "May I come in?"

Emily stared in silence. He saw her chest rise with a deep breath and her gaze drop to the casserole he carried in his hands.

"You brought this over," he told her, lifting the dish that was part of the care package she had left at his house. "I was hoping you'd share it with me."

He let the invitation dangle. Words had come so easily to him once. Glib words, careful words, probing questions, difficult answers—they had rolled off his tongue whenever he needed them. Now he needed an apology, and it was stuck in his throat.

He met her gaze squarely and gave a slight, self-condemning shake of his head.

"I'm sorry," he said simply, but with unimpeachable sincerity. "I'm sorry."

Myriad expressions crossed Emily's face, but the one that mattered most was forgiveness. When Matthew saw it, he felt grateful and, surprisingly, relieved.

Emily stepped back from the doorway, giving him room to enter. Jo skirted past them, and Emily closed the door and led the way to her kitchen.

She said nothing as she took the casserole dish and set it atop the stove. She turned on the oven to preheat, then moved to the refrigerator, while Matthew stood by with his hands in his pockets, just as silent as she. He felt tense and awkward and was relieved when finally she turned to him. "Do you still like salads?"

He nodded. "But I don't want you going to a lot of extra trouble."

"It's no trouble." She pulled vegetables out of a bin, and Matthew took a step forward.

"Can I help you?"

Bumping the refrigerator door shut with her hip, Emily shook her head. Her smile was still shy. "No, thanks. This kitchen is kind of small."

Taking that as a hint, Matthew backed out of the way.

Her kitchen was indeed compact, but it was light and airy, and if a room could look like a person, then Emily's kitchen looked like her.

Sunny yellow wallpaper with a floral pattern in rose and green made the room look like an indoor garden. She was fond of plants, he noted; they were everywhere, sitting on the cabinets and perched on stands in the corners.

Taped to her refrigerator was a crayon drawing of a house, with a stick-figure woman and what Matthew assumed were stick-figure animals playing in purple grass. "To Miss Gardiner" was written across the top in green crayon, and in blue: "I love you, Joshua Bernal, Age 6."

It looked like the young artist had spent much more time on the letters than he had on the drawing itself. Matthew smiled at the orange hair shooting out of the stick woman's head. Clearly, the drawing was meant to depict Emily in front of her cottage.

"One of your admirers?" He pointed to the square paper.

"Oh." She looked toward the refrigerator, nodded, and at last a real smile relaxed her tense features. "Josh comes to Monday afternoon story time at the library. He's planning to be an artist. Last week he checked out a book about impressionists."

"You're kidding." Matthew laughed. They were doing little more than trading pleasantries, but that was fine by him. He asked another question about the kid, just to keep the mood more relaxed.

"Is he that good a reader at his age?"

"He's good." The fondness in her expression grew. "But he isn't *that* good. He'll muddle through. His mother will probably read it to him before bedtime."

Grinning, Matthew shook his head. "And you encourage his artistic pursuits, of course. And stick figures aside, you tell him he's a wonderful artist."

In the middle of slicing a tomato, Emily nodded. "I admire artistic talent." She glanced at the drawing. Joshua's depiction of her hair made her look like she'd swallowed a firecracker. "Or artistic *desire*," she amended, smiling. "I think we should encourage it in young people."

"I remember."

His voice was low and compelling. It drew Emily's full attention. When she saw the tenderness in his expression and the steadiness of his gaze, her face grew warm. Matthew turned and moved to her breakfast nook.

An antique pine dining table was nestled into a bay window overlooking the garden.

"This is a nice home, Emily. Very pretty."

"Thank you."

She nodded. "Pretty" described her home well. It was attractive and feminine, with her grandmother Gardiner's lace doilies on the arms of her sofa, and her grandmother Triplett's old hutch filled with family china. In her bedroom there was a standard-size bed with standard-size pillows and a lovely quilt her aunt Ginny had sewn for her.

It was all very nice and very comfortable and just right for one person. But there was no clutter, no mess. She never ran out of room, or brought home paintings that would require a whole new decorating scheme, or left clothes and magazines lying around because she was too busy or too tired to put them away.

She certainly never had men standing in her breakfast nook, using up all the oxygen in her kitchen. At least, Emily was fairly certain that was happening, because standing behind him, slicing tomatoes while he stood by her table, Emily was sure she had stopped breathing.

She had pictured him in her kitchen many times, eating with her or talking to her over coffee in the morning. Always, however, she had pictured him as she remembered him, and that image was a far cry from the man who stood before her.

His shoulders were as broad as she remembered, but the blue work shirt that stretched across them hung loosely over his waist and belly, emphasizing the weight he had lost.

His hair had always been blond and thick, and he'd kept it styled conservatively above his ears. It was darker now, without its former sunny streaks, and the style was far from conservative. It waved around his face and fell well below his collar. And the golden whiskers—they were...well, scruffy, she thought. But masculine. Very masculine.

"Emily, you'd already started dinner."

"Hmm?"

"You'd already started eating." He nodded toward the plate on her table. "You should have told me."

"Oh!" Wiping her hands on a dish towel, she hurried over to the table. "No, that's all right," she said dismissively, collecting her glass of apple juice and the thin turkey sandwich she hadn't taken more than a bite out of yet.

She carried the glass and the plate to the sink, self-conscious all the while and damning her own embarrassment.

I'd rather eat with you.

She was thirty-two years old. Those simple words shouldn't be impossible for an adult woman to speak, but she couldn't squeeze them out.

"That wasn't going to be much of a dinner," Matthew commented. He slanted a look at the casserole. "You're not hungry, are you? You're just taking pity on me."

"No, I'm hungry."

She picked up the pan and slid it into the oven. Returning to her salad making with deliberate slowness, she rued the sharp kernel of desperation that made her rush the casserole into the oven before Matthew could change his mind about having dinner with her.

A little hungry, middling hungry or a lot hungry, a glass of apple juice and turkey with mayonnaise and lettuce on whole wheat was her dinner every Sunday night. On Monday she had a hamburger patty and mashed potatoes, and on Tuesday, soup with corn bread and whipped butter. Wednesdays were reserved for chicken with mushrooms and brown gravy, and Thursdays saw a return of the corn bread—this time with baked beans. On Fridays, she ate fish.

Friday was fish night not because she was religiously disciplined, but because she imagined other people eating it that night, too. She had started the ritual to forge a sense of connection to the world outside her little house. Now fish on Fridays was simply a habit.

Saturday was her only "free" day. She ate at her parents' house or invited her aunts over for dinner. She planned her lunches biweekly for a little more variety. Considering her lonely routine now, she thought she might cry into the salad bowl.

But tonight! Tonight she was having tuna casserole and company, and her heart beat in happy anticipation.

A thought hit her as she was about to slice into a cucumber. "Are *you* hungry?" she asked Matthew as she laid her paring knife on the counter. "Matthew, if you came to apologize, and you don't really want to have dinner—"

"I haven't apologized yet, Emily."

He slid one of the chairs out from her dining table and gestured to it. "Sit down, would you? I came here to explain, and I think I should stop stalling and get to it. Then, after you hear what I have to say, you can decide if you still want to have dinner with me.''

Bemused, Emily walked to the chair and sat. Matthew took the chair opposite her and settled himself. He rubbed his eyes...ran a hand over his beard... clasped both hands on top of the table. Finally he smiled, and Emily could see that he was smirking at his own reluctance to begin.

He shrugged. ''I'm not sure where to start. Emily, you are the last person in the world I should have yelled at. You don't deserve my anger, I know that. You didn't say anything this morning that was wrong...or unreasonable. I'm *honored* that you asked me to be your donor. I was angry at myself, not at you.''

He put his elbow on the table and rested his chin against his clasped hands before he spoke again, more softly this time and more slowly. ''I did want to be a father once. I wanted it so much that I ruined more than one life because of it.''

Emily shook her head. ''Wanting babies doesn't ruin lives.''

Matthew's gaze settled on a point in the distance. ''It does when you're the only one who wants them.'' He brought his hands back to the table, and Emily saw the skin whiten across his knuckles as he clenched his fists. ''Jessica was pregnant when she died. With a baby she didn't want.''

''Pregnant?'' Emily repeated the news in a whisper. ''I didn't know. Aunt Ginny never said—''

''Ginny had no idea.'' Matthew's tone grew hard. ''We didn't tell anyone about the pregnancy because we weren't getting along well at the time. I never knew from one moment to the next what Jessica was going to do. It seemed better to wait."

Emily dropped her gaze to the pine table. In the background the wall clock ticked and the oven hissed. Of all the times she had thought about Matthew and her cousin and tried to imagine the life they shared, she had never imagined such pain.

"Oh, Matthew, I wish you would have told us."

"Whom would it have helped?"

Emily answered slowly. "I don't know. Maybe all of us. If we had understood everything you were going through...if we had known what really happened, then we..."

"We what?" Matthew asked when she halted uncertainly. Irony tarnished his smile. "There was nothing you could have done."

Emily looked at him in confusion. She remembered the day she heard about the accident. She had known then, as she knew now, that there was no way for her to fully comprehend what Matthew felt, but she couldn't understand not wanting to relieve some of the pain by sharing it. Looking at Matthew now, however, at the smoky blue eyes that hid rather than revealed whatever he was thinking, she could see clearly that he shouldered his pain alone.

How she longed to reach across the table and touch him—his hand, his arm. But she had never learned how to offer a touch that was uninvited.

Her gaze dropped to his hands. There were faint smudges of wood stain on the pads of his thumbs, and his hands were deeply tanned, almost as if they were stained, too.

She imagined her fingers curling comfortingly around his, but her own hands stayed uselessly in her lap.

"Will you tell me about it?" Her soft plea drew his look. "As much of it as you can."

Matthew raised his gaze to Emily's and felt his gut clench. "The truth doesn't always help, Emily."

"I'd like to hear it."

Standing, he walked across the room, away from Emily and the small table that left too little space between them. His stomach trembled in a way it hadn't since he was a kid, and he understood then the one overwhelming reason he didn't want to tell her: the blame.

The blame was always there, in the back of his mind. It no longer mattered whether it was logical or not: it was so deeply etched inside him that sometimes he thought it was pressing on his soul, defying any light to come in, any darkness to seep out. Would it feel any worse if he added Emily's blame to his own?

He gazed out the window above the sink. This window, too, overlooked a small garden that had clearly been lovingly tended. The plants were green and full. There was life all around this little cottage.

In the short time he had spent with Emily today, he could see clearly that she still possessed a simple purity. She was still the gentlest person he had ever known. Here in her tiny home, time had stopped. Her world was like an old movie, with no swear words, no villain who could not be vanquished. Faith in life was practiced here, faith in the mechanics of the world; he could feel it.

How could she possibly understand the mess he had made of his life?

The tap on his shoulder was more a whisper than a touch. Still, Matthew felt himself jerk—and felt Emily jerk her hand back in response.

"You said you ruined more than one life." Her voice was cotton-soft and searching. "Why? Why do you blame yourself?"

Slowly, he turned toward her. Tension tightened his jaw, but she had asked a guileless question, and he knew it deserved a guileless answer.

"My relationship with Jessica was over long before she died, Emily." Forced through a tight throat, his words sounded hoarse. "I asked her for a divorce five months before she got pregnant."

Bald shock froze Emily's features, but Matthew made himself continue. "We didn't have a marriage, anymore," he stated flatly, "we had a social life. There was always an event Jessica couldn't miss. It didn't matter what the occasion was as long as it gave her the chance to get out of the house, or the opportunity to invite people in. The one thing she couldn't stand was being alone."

"Was she alone much?" Emily colored immediately after asking the question. It sounded censorious.

"I meant alone with me," Matthew corrected wryly. "Nothing bored her more than an evening home with her husband. After a while, nothing bored me more than one of her gala evenings out."

He turned from the window. "Neither of us had been happy for a long time. We started fighting. I refused to go out; she refused to stay in." He shook his head. "Finally one night, I told her I was through with the life we were living. Our relationship, the law I was practicing—it all seemed like a dead end to me. We weren't building anything...except a bigger bank account."

Matthew's eyes narrowed. He remembered the evening with crystal clarity. It had been their worst fight. Disgusted with the sham his life had become, he had told his wife that he intended to leave Boston and his law practice and return to True. The mere prospect had horrified Jessica. They'd argued bitterly and futilely until finally Matthew had brought up divorce.

Jessica had stopped fighting instantly. Cajoling and wheedling, she had tried to make him see that they had a good life, a life their family and friends back in Oregon envied.

Matthew had seen their marriage clearly then, had seen that all that was left of their relationship was what they could do for each other. So he had struck a bargain.

"I agreed to stay in Boston," he told Emily. "I agreed to stay in the marriage...if she would agree to have a baby."

"And she did agree," Emily said softly.

"With the greatest reluctance. I kept pushing her." The muscles in his jaw tensed as he remembered the anger, the ultimatums, the fact that his only child had been conceived in bitterness.

"The only reason I made love to my wife was to conceive a child. The only reason she made love to me was to keep the life she enjoyed. I think for that reason alone we were both relieved when we learned she was pregnant."

He stared over Emily's head. "The night Jessica died, I refused an invitation to a benefit. She was furious when she found out. She started yelling...I started yelling. We were both out of control. She was three months pregnant by this time, and I realized that night that all I really wanted was the baby.'' Matthew's voice was raw with self-recrimination.

"When she locked herself in the bedroom, I was relieved. I went to the guest room and shut the door. I never even heard her leave.'' He stated the facts bleakly, flatly. "It was 2.00 a.m. when they found her. She was on her way back from the party. Apparently she'd been driving too quickly and miscalculated a curve. There were skid marks—'' His jaw tensed, but this time he couldn't mask the pain in his eyes. "She was thirty-two years old and pregnant with a baby I'd practically blackmailed her to have.''

For a moment, Matthew closed his eyes. When he opened them and spoke again, his voice was a fierce and ragged whisper.

"Jessica wasn't strong enough to leave. I should have been. I had no right to bring a child into a loveless relationship. I had no right.''

And you don't want to do it again. Sadness pressed heavily on Emily's heart. She ached for the man before her, for her cousin and their child, and for herself.

Once more this evening, she stretched beyond her usual boundaries to place a hand lightly, tentatively on his sleeve.

"*You* would have been right for your child, Matthew.'' She spoke with quiet assurance. "You would be such a good father.''

Matthew looked down at the hand on his sleeve. It was delicate and pale. It trembled. He raised his eyes to Emily's face and found no condemnation, no blame or reproach. He saw only sadness and caring, a profound and guileless caring.

He shook his head. After the failure he had made of his marriage, he thought it unfair to accept comfort from his wife's family. Now he steeled himself against his need for comfort.

"You don't owe me your loyalty," he told her. "Jessica was your cousin."

Impulsively, Emily grabbed his hand in both of hers. "Matthew, I grieved for Jessica once, and now I'll do it again, but don't ask me to hold either of you responsible. It might make you feel better, but it would make me feel much worse."

His eyes dropped to their joined hands. With a self-conscious duck of her head, Emily let go. Matthew lowered his head, too.

It had been a year and a half since he'd felt like he had any connection to this planet, any tie to another human being. His sense of isolation had been a prison he'd accepted. It had never occurred to him that someone he had known all his life could hold the key. Until this moment, he hadn't been certain that there *was* a key.

"Thank you." He lifted his hand to Emily's face, letting his fingertips brush softly along her temples. "Don't ever change."

They stood quietly for a moment. Matthew took a step away. "I think I'd better go."

"No, please don't." Emily pushed her hair behind her ears and searched for a way to ease the tension. Smiling appealingly, she shrugged. "I don't want to be left alone with one of my aunt's tuna casseroles. They scare me."

Matthew raised a golden brow. "They scare you?"

Emily nodded. "Yes. She puts in these huge, hard chunks of cheddar cheese that never melt." She solemnly shook her head. "It doesn't matter how long you cook it. And once when she ran out of corn flakes, she sprinkled raisin bran over the top. If I have to eat it by myself, I might have an anxiety attack."

Matthew laughed. For the second time that day, he felt her humor like a balm, warming his chest, relaxing his muscles. He looked at Emily and allowed his gratitude to shine freely in his eyes. "I happen to like huge hard chunks of cheddar cheese in my tuna casserole."

Emily's smile brightened the small kitchen.

Somewhere deep inside of Matthew, an accustomed but burdensome heaviness was beginning to ease.

And somewhere deep inside of Emily, an unaccustomed but wonderful fullness was beginning to grow.

Chapter Four

"Been a hell of a reunion so far, hasn't it?" Matthew leaned a hip against the counter. "Oops. Sorry."

"Sorry for what?" Emily took advantage of Matthew's teasing tone to put some physical distance between them. She moved aside a few steps, picked up her paring knife and resumed slicing vegetables.

"Sorry I said 'hell.' I know you don't swear."

She rested her hand on the counter and turned to look at him. "I swear... occasionally."

White teeth beamed between mustache and beard. "You do not."

Her brows drew together and her lips puckered. She could hardly argue the point. Everyone in town knew that Miss Gardiner never swore. There were plenty of words in the English language that were both colorful and clean. But somehow today that viewpoint made her feel like a spinster librarian. The fact that she *was* a spinster librarian made her feel worse.

"Emily—" Matthew laughed at her pinched expression "—it wasn't an insult."

"Then why does it sound like one? Whenever someone says, 'Sorry, I forgot you don't swear'—and they're *grinning* when they say it—it sounds like an insult." She hacked into a perfectly innocent bell pepper.

Before she could make another mad slice, Matthew's hand covered hers.

"How about if I make the salad and you make the dessert?"

He'd tempered his grin and now there was an almost boyish smile on his lips and in those movie-idol eyes. It was his hand, though, that captured Emily's complete attention. The way it looked covering her much smaller, paler hand, and the way it felt sent a shock of heat zinging through her.

"Dessert?" she repeated thickly.

He nodded. "I could have brought the Jello-O mold—" the boyish smile grew charming "—but I have this memory of peanut-butter cookies. Do you still make them?"

"Yes." She often made them for story hour at the library.

He raised a brow. "Any chance I might get lucky? If I slice the bell pepper?"

His grin persuaded her. She laid the paring knife on the counter, slipping her hand from beneath his.

They worked in silence for a time, Matthew slicing vegetables, and Emily gathering the ingredients for the cookies she'd been baking since she was ten.

"Remember when you made these cookies for the Fourth of July, so we'd have something to eat while we watched the fireworks?"

Emily paused in her attempt to twist the lid off a fresh jar of peanut butter. "Yes, I remember." She frowned reprovingly. "I remember because you ate every cookie before I had a chance to taste even one."

Smiling broadly, he pulled the jar out of her hands. "Funny, that's why I remember it, too. I don't know why you were so crabby about it—you got to eat the dough."

"Oh, no, you should never eat raw dough," she informed him, truly concerned. "The eggs could carry the salmonella bacteria, and if they're not cooked yet—"

"Emily, Emily." Matthew laughed as he gave the lid one quick, hard twist, popping it open. "Do you mean to tell me you've never eaten raw cookie dough?"

He plucked a stalk of celery from the bunch Emily had placed on the counter and dipped it into the peanut butter.

She watched, virtually hypnotized by the simple gesture. "No, never," she murmured.

He took a bite of the celery. "You're more disciplined than I am."

She nodded slowly. No one had ever dipped into her peanut-butter jar before.

For years, Emily had considered her food purchases to be a dead giveaway of her single status. During weekly trips to the market, she stared at the economy-size boxes of cereal and the large plastic gallons of milk the way other women looked at diamonds in jewelry store windows. Her favorite, though, her absolute favorite product in the whole market, was a five-pound container of peanut butter. She would finger the broad plastic lid and imagine needing so much, enough for sandwiches and cookies and snacks—enough for a family.

All her food came in small packages, and it all stayed neatly wrapped, lids closed tightly, lunch meats wrapped carefully. There were no sticky fingerprints on her refrigerator door.

Now Emily stared into the peanut butter, saw the single, haphazard swipe taken out of it and thought she might bronze the jar.

"Sorry, I guess I should have asked first."

She looked up dazedly. "What?"

Matthew gestured at the jar. "Bad habit. Next thing you know I'll be drinking your milk straight from the carton."

With great effort, Emily checked the urge to go to her refrigerator and get the milk. The problem with her life was that everyone in it believed they had to ask politely when they wanted or needed something. No one was on intimate enough terms with her to simply assume anything.

She put the peanut butter on the counter, pulled a measuring cup out of the cabinet, then thought better of it and returned the cup to its shelf. She'd been making these cookies for twenty years; she knew how much peanut butter she had to use, how many sticks of butter, how much flour she would need to make the batter the right consistency.

For once, she would wing it!

A small smile tugged her lips. She was living positively dangerously today.

"What's funny?"

Emily looked over at Matthew. He was slicing a carrot. She shook her head to tell him that what she'd been thinking wasn't worth talking about and asked instead, "Do you ever make cookies for yourself?"

He laughed. "No. All cookies were supplied by our housekeeper, who, I am certain, purchased them at a very expensive bakery. They usually had white chocolate. I hate white chocolate."

"Why didn't you tell her?"

"I did. The alternatives were just as bad. How the hell—" He caught himself, grinned and continued. "How can you relax when you're eating a cookie with a design on it? Have you ever had a cappuccino cookie?"

Emily giggled. "I don't think so."

"You haven't missed much. I always thought the minute I had a kid, I'd buy a whole case of Oreos, so he'd never have to look at a marmalade drop."

"Is that what you wanted—a son?"

Matthew looked up, bemused.

"You said *he*," Emily pointed out quietly.

"Did I?" He shook his head slowly. That easy reference was the first mention of a child he'd been able to make in more than a year. "I don't think I consciously had a preference. But when I pictured it all . . . yeah, I guess I saw myself with a son."

Rubbing his beard, he glanced at her contemplatively. "How about you? Boy or girl?"

"A girl, I think." Emily had been thinking about it for some time, and saying it aloud felt good; it made the intention seem real. "I love little boys, too, but I think I understand girls better. I'm more equipped to raise a daughter on my own."

She paused, noting the interest in his eyes, appreciating his willingness not only to refer to her plans, but to take them seriously.

"Matthew," she ventured, taking the bull by the horns, "if I'd had any idea that you lost a child, I never would have mentioned— I mean, I never would have asked—" Shaking her head, she met his eyes and tried again. "I was so nervous this morning, I just blurted it out. I must have seemed rather glib to you."

Matthew accepted the apology with a smile.

He put all the salad ingredients into a bowl, took it upon himself to look in her refrigerator for a bottle of dressing and brought everything to the table.

Abandoning her cookie ingredients for the moment, Emily pulled out plates and silverware and joined him at the table. When Matthew sat down, she followed suit.

He placed his napkin on his lap, opened the bottle of dressing and handed it to her. "You're really eager to raise a child on your own?"

"I'm really eager to love a child, and I'm *willing* to raise her—or him—on my own." She had considered this question so many times, but she'd never discussed it with anyone. "I think it's preferable for a child to have two parents. And I would like to be part of a traditional family. But that isn't happening to me, and I don't want to wait in vain and miss having a child altogether."

"You're only—what? Thirty, thirty-one? You still have a lot of time to meet someone."

"I'm thirty-two, but that isn't the point."

As they spoke, they started on their salads, and Emily was surprised to discover that she could sit across a dinner table and discuss something so very personal with an ease she usually reserved for topics like the weather.

"When I was researching the whole subject of having a baby alone, I read a book that had a list of questions in the back. An 'Are-you-doing-this-for-all-the-right-reasons' test. It asked things like 'Are you lonely? Is there a hole in your life you think a child can fill?'" She toyed with her salad a moment, then put down her fork and bravely raised her eyes to Matthew's.

"I truly believe I have a lot to offer a child. I think I'll be a good mother. But there *is* a hole." Her brow furrowed. "I've gone along in my life doing what everyone expected of me for so long, or doing what seemed easy, I suppose. Taking the path of least resistance. Lately I've begun to feel..." She smiled self-consciously. "This is hard to explain, but I've begun to feel like I'm living somebody else's life. Like I've been waiting for years for somebody to come along and notice that I'm stuck in the mud and then help pull me out of it. But then I realized I'm the only one who has to notice that I'm stuck. I can do something for myself, *by* myself, if I have to."

She leaned forward in her chair. "I'm not having a baby because I'm bored. But I'm not going to wait any longer because I'm scared."

Matthew regarded her intently. "*Are* you scared?"

Reluctantly, Emily nodded. "Not about having a child, but about the way I'm going to do it. I'm a little worried about how people might react. This is such a conservative town."

Matthew's jaw tensed. "The hell with them, if it's what you want. Have you told anyone about it yet?"

"I told you." She rose from the table. "I'd better check on dinner."

She was peering into the oven when he stood and crossed to her. Glimpsing the leg of his jeans out of the corner of her eye, Emily pulled out the casserole and set it on top of the stove. Matthew reached in front of her to close the oven door.

"I'm grateful that you asked me to be the donor, Emily." His voice was low and gravelly. "I'm grateful and I'm flattered. And I'm sorry I can't help you."

The regret and the finality in his tone almost proved to be Emily's undoing. For just a moment when he said that he was grateful, she had hoped again.

Giving him what she prayed was a comfortably resigned smile, Emily headed for the table with the casserole and an eagerness completely unbefitting her aunt's cooking.

"We'd better eat," she said brightly. "Once Aunt Tillie's casseroles cool, they start to congeal."

She took her seat and put her napkin in her lap.

"Em." Matthew remained standing. "I can't help you with the actual process of having a child, but I can be your friend while you go through it. And I would like that," he said quietly. "I would like that very much."

Emily reached for the serving spoon.

The "process" could take as long as six months and then, God willing, there would be nine months of pregnancy... and a whole lifetime of rearing and loving. She didn't know how long he intended to stay in True, but she knew that, at best, he would share only a fraction of the experience with her. Still, a fraction shared with a friend would be better than the whole thing experienced alone, and she had no idea how her family was going to react.

She smiled more genuinely and reached for Matthew's plate. "I'd like it, too."

An hour after Matthew left, Emily was sitting on her couch with Jo by her feet. When the little cat mewed, Emily patted her knees.

"Come on up."

Jo popped onto her mistress's lap, made an exploratory circle and settled herself cozily.

"We had company tonight, didn't we, Jo-Jo?" Emily crooned, stroking the cat's long fur. Jo purred and rubbed the top of her head against Emily's knee.

Matthew hadn't stayed long after dinner. The cookies would have to wait until another evening—and there *would* be other evenings with Matthew Carter, Emily was sure. As long as he was in town, his friendship would be hers for the asking.

Anticipation built in Emily's chest; she tingled with the desire for tonight to be over and a new day to begin. When was the last time she had felt this way?

"He's a friend—*only* a friend," she reminded herself adamantly, but a moment later, she imagined that Jo's hair was Matthew's, and as she twirled it around her finger, she pictured Matthew looking up at her, his head in her lap. What would they do if they were together every evening as a couple, making plans, choosing activities together?

Emily felt drowsy, hypnotized by the blue eyes she imagined gazing up at her, captured by the *way* she imagined them gazing at her.

"Do you still want to make cookies?" she would ask as her fingers played through his golden hair.

"No." As if the moment were real, she saw his beautiful lips curve into a smile. *"I want something, but not cookies."*

He reached for her, his fingers buried in her hair, his palm warm and hard against the side of her face. She felt the insistence of his pull as he drew her down... down... down for his kiss...

"Miaaow!" Jo rolled onto her back, swiping at Emily's hand and battling her nose with her paws. She graciously refrained from extending her claws for the attack, but her displeasure was clear. Emily jerked back and the little cat scurried off her lap.

"Rrrriaow." Jo shot a highly irritated, protracted glare at her mistress, then began to wash herself.

Emily brought a hand to her forehead. "Oh, God, what am I doing?"

She was a thirty-two-year-old woman, for heaven's sake! Her fantasy days were over, or they should have been.

Pushing herself from the couch with a determination that made Jo run for cover, Emily walked purposefully to her bedroom. She went to her vanity table, opened the middle drawer and pulled out the papers she had stored there almost a month ago.

The top page was an information sheet; the following pages formed a lengthy health questionnaire. There was a doctor's name, an address and a phone number at the top of each sheet. The graphic design that headed the pages was the silhouette of a woman with her head bowed over an infant. So far, the questionnaire was blank.

For a long moment, Emily stared at the papers. Then she crossed to her nightstand, picked up the pen by her phone and sat down on the bed to fill out the forms the alternative insemination clinic had sent her.

Chapter Five

As Matthew walked up the path to his father's home, reluctance slowed his every step.

Five years ago when Matthew's mother died, he and his father had lost not only a beloved family member, but their referee, as well. Father and son had not had a relaxed conversation since.

Tom Carter was an old-fashioned man. That was the generous explanation for his behavior. Matthew supposed that in pop-psychology terms, his father would be called passive-aggressive. He handled his family the way he handled his business: he was the boss. He had expectations and he wanted them to be met without excuses. But Tom Carter was no tyrant. He was kind; he was soft-spoken. To Matthew's knowledge no one had ever let his father down, chiefly because his expectations were so damn *reasonable*. Tom himself was so damn reasonable that it was hard for most people to get or stay angry at him—at least, as angry as one needed to be in order to break away.

Matthew paused with one boot on the top step of the porch and one hand locked in a fierce grip around the railing. If he thought about his mother, about Jessica, about Harvard Law School, about all of the wasted years living his father's dream, he would never make it to the front door.

Moving onto the porch, his boots falling heavily on the cracked and weathered wood, he rang the bell. It was eight o'clock in the morning, a half hour before Tom would leave for work. It didn't take long for him to answer the door.

Standing on the other side of the threshold, Matthew's father blinked several times behind his glasses.

"Matthew?" Tom Carter cocked his head, like the dog in the old RCA Victrola ad. He peered at his only child, looking uncertainly at the beard and long hair and at the stained work clothes.

Matthew smiled, but the smile was for himself, not his father. "In the flesh, Dad. May I come in?"

"Well, sure, sure." Tom stepped back from the doorway. "I heard you were back in town, but I didn't expect—" He stopped himself, waited for Matthew to enter and closed the door. "Go on into the kitchen. I have breakfast cooking."

Silently, Matthew led the way through the house. It hadn't changed a bit since his childhood.

The kitchen still had the old vine-patterned wallpaper his mother had put up twenty years ago. The teakettle was still copper. Matthew leaned against the tiled counter.

"Sit down," his father instructed, attending to the small pot on the stove. "I'll start another pot of oatmeal."

"Not for me, thank you," Matthew declined.

"Yes, don't be silly. I'll throw on a few more slices of bacon and a couple pieces of toast. I've got a good loaf of bread here." Tom moved to the refrigerator and pulled out the package of bacon he bought every Sunday night when he did his marketing for the week.

"I've already eaten."

Tom continued with his preparations as though his offer of breakfast had been enthusiastically accepted. "This is without a doubt," he stated, "the finest bacon in the world. Look at that." He held up a piece for Matthew's inspection. "Did you ever see bacon that lean?"

Matthew spoke to his father on major holidays, on birthdays and on Father's Day. They had not seen each other since Jessica's funeral. And yet somehow for them, bacon seemed a logical topic.

"It's lean all right." Matthew glowered at the slimy strip, wondering why he had come.

Ignoble as it was, his original intention had been to avoid seeing his father for as long as he could. But after talking to Emily last night, he'd had some vague notion of coming here and telling Tom the truth—the truth about himself and Jessica, the truth about the resentment he'd been carrying all these years, the bald truth about his fury at the man he had tried throughout his youth and through too much of his adulthood to please.

Tom put bread in the toaster and bacon in the pan. He stood with his back to the son he hadn't seen in over a year and a half, and—worse than saying nothing—he began chattering like a squirrel.

Great bacon...terrific bread...only one good way to cook oatmeal.

He blathered about everything; he said absolutely nothing, and all in the attempt to keep silence—or any real conversation—at bay.

By the time they started eating, Matthew was so filled with tension, he could barely swallow a bite of the breakfast his father had prepared. Tom, on the other hand, dug in with fair enthusiasm.

"So, how long you staying, son?"

"Indefinitely."

"Indefinitely?" Tom looked up. He held a piece of well-done bacon in his left hand and a large cereal spoon in his right. From behind his glasses, he blinked curiously at his son. "How do the boys in the office take to that?"

Matthew thought of the senior female partner and how she would feel about being referred to as one of "the boys." He smiled. "They're taking to it all right."

"When do they expect you back?"

Matthew tasted the hot cereal in the bowl before him and reached for the sugar. He never ate oatmeal anymore. Now it sent him straight back to high school mornings, sitting across the table from his father while his mother buzzed around the kitchen, preparing their lunches. Tom would ask Matthew about school and football practice, and Matthew would show his father any new college brochures he'd received.

"They don't."

Tom stopped eating. "Son, you weren't let go, were you?" Matthew could see clearly the shock and the horror that lay just behind the concern etched on his father's face.

"No, Dad," he reassured gently, "I wasn't fired."

"Thank the Lord," Tom muttered, pressing a knife into the margarine. "That's a blot you don't want on your record. Sometimes it can't be helped, of course, but I say most dismissals can be avoided if you're doing your best."

Matthew dragged a spoon through his oatmeal. "Well, I'm not being fired, Dad." Giving up on the cereal, he dropped the spoon and picked up his coffee. He inhaled the familiar aroma of the French roast his father had been using for years and said with as little challenge in his voice as he could manage, "I'm resigning."

Beneath the reddened, aged skin of his neck, Tom Carter's Adam's apple bobbed with several nervous swallows. "You've resigned from the firm?"

"Not formally," Matthew admitted. "Not yet, but—"

"Well, I'm glad to hear that." Tom nodded briskly. "Seems to me we've had this conversation a time or two before."

Matthew smiled grimly. "Seems like it," he agreed. "But I'm not here to discuss it this time, Dad. I took time off so I could make a decision, and I have. The fact is I should have done this years ago."

It would have been so much easier to accept the aching disappointment on his father's face had Matthew not been aware of the sacrifices his parents had made to send him to college and to law school. Tom Carter was too good a man to remind his son of that fact, but he was not superhuman and he could no more keep the ache from showing in his eyes than he could eradicate it from his heart.

"In this economy, Matthew?" Tom rested his elbows on the table. "Are you going to go to another firm?" He didn't need his son's answer. "Do you know what you're doing?" The hand holding the piece of toast started to shake. "You've never struggled to put food on the table. What will you have to offer your family? This is about the wood again, isn't it?"

"No," Matthew answered tightly, trying not to rise to the way his father said *the wood*. "It's about me. It's about living a life that has some meaning for me."

Fire leapt in the old man's eyes. "Putting food on the table has no meaning for you? Providing for your family has no meaning?"

"I don't have a family." Matthew's jaw clenched. Damn it, he did not want to have this conversation again!

"Dad," he said, forcing himself to speak as calmly as he could, "we've got to get clear about when we're talking about me and when we're talking about you. I'm not denying the meaning of your life. I just want to live more simply than I was living in Boston. That's not meant to be an assault on your values. It's a statement about mine."

Tension thinned Tom's lips, making the age lines around his mouth stand out more clearly than ever before. "God gives a man a fine mind and a good education," he said, "that's not something to waste."

"He gave me two good hands, too."

"The wood ought to be a hobby, son! You have responsibilities. You'll marry again someday—"

"I doubt it."

"Don't talk foolishness!"

Across the table tension stretched between father and son like rubber bands ready to snap.

"I'm not happy." They were words Matthew had not planned to say, but they rose from his gut.

Tom shook his head. "A man makes his happiness."

"That's what I'm doing." Standing, Matthew flung his napkin onto the table. "That is what I'm trying to do."

"You had a good life. You could have that again, you—"

"I had nothing!" Matthew leaned over the table. His palms came down so hard, the dishes shook. "Why can't you get it through that thick head of yours? All I had was a lie. Jessica was miserable, I was miserable. *You* would have been happy in Boston, not me. Lies kill, Dad, can you understand *that?* Lies kill."

Time stopped for both men. The tension hung thick and silent between them.

Tom remained seated, appearing more confused and frustrated than he was angry. He was no closer to understanding his son now than he had been a year ago or two years ago or fifteen. How a man could choose a life no better than the one he'd been born with... That would never make sense to him. Never.

Matthew watched his father blinking up at him from behind glasses that had turned into bifocals and then trifocals over the years. *This is what I wanted,* he realized with a fullness in his gut that nearly made him sick. *This is how I wanted him to look. Confused and frustrated... and sorry for something he doesn't even understand.*

The pain in the room was palpable. To an extent, both men had their say. Neither of them felt better for it and neither of them knew what to say next.

They stared at each other, bound by emotions that would outlast time and yet helpless to make this one moment feel better.

Matthew swallowed against the pain that was rising in his throat. He straightened from the table. When he spoke, his voice was hoarse. "I've got to go. I'll call you... maybe next week...."

Tom blinked rapidly behind his glasses. He nodded, but remained seated and said nothing as Matthew turned and walked out of the house.

"Miss Gardiner, I gotta go bad an' I can't get into the bathro-o-o-om!"

Taylor Gordon, seven years old, held on to the waistband of his jeans and squirmed while he whined.

Emily sighed heavily, brushed a stray hair that had fallen out of her French twist and prayed for patience. Monday story hour had been over for twenty minutes and most of the children were still in the library, waiting to be picked up.

"You went to the rest room fifteen minutes ago, Taylor. What do you mean you can't get in?"

"Paul Farrar is in there, Miss Gardiner, and he's blocking the do-o-or!"

"Blocking the door," Emily muttered, rising from her chair and heading for the boys' room. Mondays were always busy and usually stressful, but this particular Monday had shown no mercy.

Taylor loped after her, still clutching his pants, but speaking with less whine and more enthusiasm for the trouble ahead as they approached the bathroom.

"Paul's barricadin' the door with his foot, Miss Gardiner, and he says he's not comin' out an' he's not lettin' anyone in until Julie the troll goes home!"

Emily stopped short. "Taylor, what did I tell you about calling people mean names?"

Taylor's bottom lip jutted. "*I* didn't call her a troll—Paul did." The boy's brown eyes lit enthusiastically again. "He's not comin' out because Julie said she's gonna kiss him the next time she sees him!"

Emily shook her head and continued to the rest room. At least Julie was showing some initiative in getting her man.

The library closed at six o'clock, but it was almost seven before Emily was able to finish her work and leave for the night. Her back and hip were aching from the extra work created when her shelver called in sick with a cold. Her limp, always a little worse at the end of the day, was more pronounced than usual.

She had no intention of going straight home, however. Early this morning, she had dropped her medical forms in the mail. The ball was rolling, and now she was ready for the next step: she was going to tell her family about her plans.

After speaking with Matthew last night, she knew that she could not sneak and skulk her way through this. She wanted to go forward with pride and with some support, if that was possible. Matthew would not be here forever, but her family would.

She arrived at her parents' home as they were sitting down to dessert and TV in the living room.

Rose Gardiner broke into a wide, pleased smile when she saw her daughter. "Emily! You're in time for peach pie. I wish you'd have called to say you were coming. We had kielbasa and sauerkraut for dinner, but I let your father eat the last sausage!''

While Rose talked, she ushered Emily to the living room. Lil and Tillie were seated on the sofa, and Emily's father, Ernest, was in his favorite chair, a plate of pie in his hands.

"Hello, Dolly." Ernest glanced up from the television to smile at his daughter.

"Hi, Daddy."

"Emily, sit next to your aunts, dear. I'll cut you some pie."

"No thanks, Mom." Emily sat on the couch and hoped she could marshal her family into some semblance of coherence. *Vague* described most of her relatives on a good day.

"I came to talk to you about something specific," she stated as Rose took her seat in a chair across from her husband.

Tillie leaned eagerly toward her great-niece. "Which of us did you want to talk to, Emily dear?"

Lil jabbed her sister in the ribs. "She came to talk to her parents." To Emily she said, "We'll just go up to our room."

"No, you don't have to do that. I came to talk to all of you."

"Ernie, turn off the TV," Rose instructed.

Ernest looked confused. "Turn it off?"

"Yes. It doesn't have to be going all the time."

"Emmy, you want me to turn off the TV?" Ernest turned to his daughter.

"Just for a little while, Dad, yes."

Shrugging, Ernest pressed the remote he kept on the arm of his chair. Four pairs of eyes turned toward

Emily. Four mouths chewed pie. Four faces held expressions that were interested but utterly unwitting.

How could she slide gracefully into this discussion?

Emily smiled. "I'm going to be thirty-three in August, you know," she began, then paused hesitantly.

They smiled back and nodded.

"Thirty-three is not *old*," Emily continued, groping for a segue. "In respect to many things, thirty-three is still young."

"In respect to *us*, it's still infantile," Lilly whispered loudly to her sister. Tillie scowled.

"But," Emily went on, "I can't ignore the fact that years are passing. Important years. Years I don't want to waste. And so, turning thirty-three in August has taken on a new significance."

Rose nodded at her daughter, her brow furrowed in deep thought. Her expression cleared quite suddenly, and she wagged her head broadly. "Emily, Emily, oh, how could I have been so neglectful? You want a birthday party!" Rose deposited her pie on the coffee table. "Is that what you're trying to tell us, darling? Oh, you poor sweetheart, you haven't had a birthday party since you were a little girl, and now you have to ask for one." She snatched up the pen she'd been using for her crossword puzzle. "We can start planning it right away. Let's see, August is how many months away?" She tapped four fingers against her thumb.

"No, Mom—"

Tillie clasped her hands. "We could make it a surprise party!"

"Now how are we going to do that? Emily's right here." Lil scowled at her sister. "Twit."

"If you dare to call me names, Lilly Gardiner, I will personally see to it that you are not invited!"

"Oh, I'll be invited, all right—"

"Aunties, please," Rose admonished, shaking her head at her in-laws. "Everyone is coming to the party—"

"I don't want a party!" Emily raised her voice to be heard above the squabbling. "I want a *baby!*"

Her words fell like salt on a flame.

No one moved. Confusion filled her parents' faces. Her father tried to speak but wound up looking like a baby bird, opening and closing his mouth with no perceivable result.

Emily took a deep breath. "I want to have a baby," she restated more calmly. "I know it's surprising, and I realize the idea might take some getting used to for all of you, but it's something I've wanted for a long time."

"Emily." Rose tilted her head nervously, almost shyly at her daughter. "Do you have... Have you been seeing someone, dear? A...gentleman?"

Her mother looked at once hopeful and concerned.

"No, Mom," Emily said softly, "there's no man. I'm doing this on my own."

"On your own? Are you going to try to adopt?" Rose's pretty features, much like her daughter's, crimped distressfully. "Oh, Emmy, even if they let you adopt by yourself, how could you manage it, sweetheart? Raising a child all alone? Even if you were a completely healthy woman—"

"I *am* a healthy woman!"

The vehemence of Emily's response surprised everyone, Emily included. As a child, she had naturally bucked the idea that she had limitations; as a teenager, she had reluctantly accepted the boundaries of scoliosis; as an adult, she had at times *embraced* those boundaries, because they gave her a reason to avoid risks.

Now she was through coddling herself, and she did not want anyone else to coddle her, either. She wanted support and she wanted respect.

"I'm not going to adopt," she stated, bracing herself to use the term that could very likely send her family into group shock. "I'm going to have a baby through alternative insemination."

She used the words she had read over and over on the health forms last night. *Alternative* sounded much better than *artificial*.

But to her family, it all sounded the same. It sounded scandalous.

Emily looked around the room. Her parents seemed to be having trouble breathing: her mother was hyperventilating; her father was barely taking in any air at all. She braved a glance at her aunts, and that was where she found her surprise.

Aunt Tillie was watching her with tears in her eyes, but there was no sadness or fear in her delicate, aged face. Her expression was wistful and—unless Emily was greatly mistaken—approving.

Lil stared at her niece without tears, but her wrinkled chin was lifted and her strong, defined features bore pride.

Lilly jerked her head once in a quick, brusque nod that said clearly, *Good for you.*

"Say something, Ernest." Like a drowning person reaching for a lifeline, Rose waved a hand in her husband's direction.

Ernest looked from his wife to his daughter. He cleared his throat but couldn't manage an actual word.

Tillie filled the tense silence with a timid, halting response to the news. "Congratulations, Emily."

If possible, Rose looked even more upset than before. "Congratulations?" She looked at her daughter wild-eyed. "You haven't done this thing yet, have you?"

Emily smiled gratefully at her aunt, but Tillie was already glancing nervously down at her own hands. She lived in her nephew's house; she would never feel comfortable openly flouting Rose and Ernest.

Emily took another long breath. Although she had anticipated her parents' reactions, her discomfort was keen. It was so hard for her to disappoint the people she loved—and just as hard to be disappointed by them.

"I haven't gone through the procedure yet, no." Her voice was as steady as her emotions would allow. "But I've taken the preliminary steps. This morning I made an appointment with the doctor I'm going to be seeing."

Rose pressed a hand to her slim, pale neck. "Thank God," she said, responding only to the information that the insemination had not yet taken place. "Cancel the appointment before they get any money out of you. You can't work and raise a baby on your own! You've no idea how much energy it takes to raise a child."

"I have plenty of energy, Mom."

"Emily, be sensible. You want to work all day and then go home to that cottage and have to deal with a baby? Or a child running who-knows-where when you're tired and your back is bothering you? And pregnancy is very hard on a woman's body. No reputable doctor would consider experimenting with you!"

"Mother, no one is *experimenting* on anybody."

Ernest leaned over the arm of his chair. He spoke more calmly than Rose, but he appeared no less troubled than she. "Emmy, you won't know who the child's father is?"

"I'll know quite a bit about him, but not his name, no."

"Oh, my God." Rose shook her head disconsolately.

"This procedure is readily accepted by the medical community... and by society." *Most of society,* Emily added silently, looking at their wary faces.

She did not like confrontation. She wasn't used to making definitive statements, even regarding her own life. But she knew that peace in her future and in her child's future would depend on her ability to command respect now.

"I've already made my decision. I came here to talk to you about it, so you wouldn't feel like you were being taken by surprise. I want you to know how excited I am about this." *I want you to know how frightened I am, too. I want you to hold my hand and tell me you'll knit booties... build a swing set....*

But Emily could not make herself say any more, not with their disappointment and their anxiety drawn so plainly on their faces. They thought they knew her better than she knew herself. They saw her limitations and they wanted to protect her, but they did not see her strength.

Aunt Tillie, as shy and cautious as a sparrow, leaned into the silence, offering comfort the only way she knew how. "Are you sure you wouldn't like some pie, dear?"

Emily patted Tillie's thin, nervous fingers. "No, thank you." She mustered a smile for the woman whose life she was trying so hard not to emulate.

When Emily rose from the couch, her mother stood too. "Why don't you stay? We—we'll watch some TV. We don't have to talk about this anymore right now."

Rose's face was so pained that Emily felt her throat and eyes burn with tears. She shook her head.

"I need to get home. I have to...feed Jo." She turned to the door, knowing they were watching her.

As she walked out of the house, she took care to make each step as smooth and steady as possible. The ache in her back and hip was minimal compared to the ache in her heart.

Emily's mood darkened on the short drive back to her cottage. The pain in her back was growing more insistent, and self-doubt was worming into her mind. What if she really couldn't run after a toddler on a bad-back day like this one? What if she didn't have the stamina or the patience to play with her own child?

Frustrated by her thoughts and furious that she was allowing her own conviction to waver, Emily stopped the car hard in front of the cottage, slammed the door and limped up to the porch, allowing her good leg to fall heavily on each step.

She didn't even notice the Jeep parked alongside the house.

In the shadows, Matthew leaned against the porch rail. He came forward as Emily fumbled the key in the lock. "Here, let me do that."

"Oh!" Jumping back when she saw a hand other than her own reach for the doorknob, Emily swung her purse at her surprise guest. It connected a moment before she recognized Matthew. "What are you doing!"

Matthew grasped her shoulders to steady her as she put a hand to her chest. "I'm sorry, Emily, I didn't mean to scare you. I wasn't thinking."

"I'll say." The woman who rarely raised her voice growled at her friend. Pulling back, she grabbed her house key and opened the door herself. She limped over the threshold and slapped the light on in the entry.

"You live in a big city—I can't believe you think it's funny to sneak up on people."

"I don't think it's funny." Matthew had been waiting at her cottage for almost two hours. He'd gone for a couple of walks, sat by the creek, told himself several times to give up and go home, but his meeting with his father was burning inside him, and when he'd thought of a way to soothe himself, he'd thought of Emily.

He'd come to the creek often in his youth to relax with her after a bad football game or a miserable exam or a fight with Jessica—anytime he had needed a break, a place to do nothing but breathe.

"What's the matter with you tonight?" He watched Emily trudge into the living room, her weight falling heavily onto her strong left leg with each step.

He'd watched her get out of her car and walk up the porch steps with the same difficulty; the distraction had made him forget to announce himself.

Without being invited, he followed her into the house.

Emily tossed her purse on the coffee table, called for Jo and sank onto the couch. Matthew came to stand in front of her.

"Are you all right, Em?"

"I'm fine."

"You're limping."

"I've always limped. You just noticed?"

The moment the sarcastic words passed her lips, Emily regretted them.

Matthew sat down beside her.

In all the time he'd known her, Emily had never expressed bitterness. She had never had fits of temper. As far as he knew, Emily saw two sides of every issue, and they were both the bright side. Now, because temper was so rare in the woman he remembered, he found her bad mood intriguing.

"I saw you having trouble with the porch steps. Did something happen today?"

Wearily, Emily shook her head. "It's just been a long day." Jo appeared, rubbing against her mistress's legs. Emily rose. "Excuse me, I have to feed Jo."

Matthew stood with her. "I'll do it." He took hold of her wrist and held her stationary while he brushed passed her. "You sit back down."

Taken by surprise, Emily stared after him. "You don't know where anything is." She started forward.

Matthew turned, blocking her path. "I'll find it. Go sit down. Rest your leg."

He turned toward the kitchen again. Glancing between her mistress and the man, Jo followed the human who was moving in the direction of the food. Once more, Emily started to follow.

"There is nothing wrong with my leg!"

In her own mind, physical disabilities were not flaws. At the same time, she believed that other people *did* perceive her limp to be a defect, an impairment that rendered her less whole, less attractive, less capable than others. And, certainly, tonight she had suffered through enough references to the condition of her body to last her a lifetime.

"I can take care of my own cat," she informed Matthew on a growl as she marched after him, her back and hip aching with every step. "I'm perfectly capable of taking care of whatever has to be done around here, thank you—now and in the future. I do not need you to feed my cat or monitor my health. I'm not crippled."

"Crippled!" Matthew swung around, a furious scowl darkening his brow. "I'm being accused of thinking you're crippled because I offered to feed your cat? What the hell kind of logic is that?" He rubbed a hand over his face. "Look, Emily, I'm tired, you're tired. We've obviously had a long day, but physically you're more exhausted than I am, so for God's sake, *sit down!*"

His final words were a bark. They faced off until poor, hungry Jo meowed as if she was sure she would never be fed again. Matthew turned and stalked off to the kitchen. Silently, Emily watched him go.

She sat on the couch and listened to him searching her cabinets for cat food. She heard the electric can opener humming its way around a lid, and she heard the eager meow Jo always gave as her dinner was being served. Several minutes passed. Matthew returned bearing two steaming mugs.

"Tea," he said, setting the mugs on the coffee table. "All right?"

Emily nodded. She felt guilty, embarrassed and miserable. "Thank you."

They sat quietly for a moment. Matthew leaned forward, resting his elbow on his thighs. "I had a lousy day, too," he said, staring at the rug. "That's why I came over."

"What happened?"

He shook his head. "We can talk about it later. I should have waited and called first. Here." He reached over, picked up a mug of tea and placed it in her hands.

She thanked him again, then opened her mouth to apologize for the way she was acting this evening. Before a syllable came out, Emily stopped, her eyes widening abruptly as fingers—Matthew's fingers—curled around her neck. He started massaging.

"What are you doing?"

"Shh." He raised his other hand to her shoulder and turned her slightly away from him. Both his thumbs began moving in long, slow circles at the base of her neck. "Relax," he told her. While his thumbs moved on the back of her neck, his fingers rested along her collarbone.

Relax? She was wearing a scoop-necked blouse. His hands were on her skin. The last time a man's hands had been on her bare neck, she'd had strep throat and old Dr. Naditch had been checking her lymph glands.

Emily perched on the end of the sofa cushion, her back ramrod straight.

"Uh, you don't have to…" she began, then snapped her jaw shut as his thumbs moved up toward her hairline.

She tried to remember if he had ever done this to her when they were younger. If he had, it must have felt a whole lot different, because *this* she would never have forgotten.

Unfortunately, instead of relaxing, she could feel herself getting stiffer.

As his hands moved down her neck to work the tops of her shoulders, she tried again to speak. "Really, I appreciate this, but—"

"Shh." He pressed harder, and she swayed forward slightly. "Just relax." His voice came low, firm and surprisingly close to her ear. "You've got knots the size of golf balls along here."

That was nothing compared to the size of the knot in her stomach, but Emily stayed silent for the rest of the massage.

Never in her sheltered life had she experienced such a sensation. Matthew's fingers smoothed and pressed and kneaded their way down her spine. Her body ebbed and flowed like the tide, moving slightly away from him as the pressure of his fingers increased, then rolling back into his hands for more.

Her eyelids lowered. Untasted, the mug of tea rested on her lap, warming the tops of her thighs.

By the time Matthew was finished, the tea had cooled, and Emily felt as weightless as a feather.

"How's your back?" He whispered to her softly, sustaining the relaxed mood. Keeping one hand on her neck, he reached for her tea with his free hand, depositing the mug on the table.

Emily stretched tentatively. When there was no pain from her small movement to the right, she leaned left. She felt nothing but a pleasing flexibility.

Turning wide, surprised eyes to Matthew, she exclaimed, "Why, it doesn't hurt at all! It feels really fine."

He smiled and nodded. "Good."

Tugging gently until she was settled comfortably against the sofa, Matthew released her and stretched his arm out along the top of the couch.

"You want to talk about what happened today?"

Emily rolled her head against the cushions. "Not if I want to stay relaxed."

He laughed and nudged her with his arm. "Talk."

Emily sighed loudly. "It was a long day at the library."

"And?"

"And then I went to see my parents. I wanted to talk to them about my decision."

"About having a baby?"

"Mmm-hmm." Emily nodded.

"It didn't go well?"

Her abbreviated smile turned wry. "It didn't go well." She glanced at him shyly. "I'm sorry I was so rude to you when I got home—"

Matthew's grin hushed her. "I told you, I was in a lousy mood, too." With one finger, he pushed a long, red wave back from her forehead. "Besides, I'd never seen Emily Gardiner in a snit before. It was very interesting."

"I wasn't in a snit." Her forehead tingled where he'd touched it. "Why were you in a lousy mood?"

"Let's do you first, then we can talk about my crummy day. I think we may have had similar problems."

Emily raised a brow wryly. "Oh? Are you planning to have a baby without a man?"

Laughing, Matthew shook his head. "I can say with confidence that I have no immediate plans in that direction. Is that what's bothering your parents? That there's no man in the picture?"

"Everything about it bothers them. They're upset that I'm doing it alone. They're upset that I'm going to use alternative insemination."

"You said that very well this time," he commended.

"I've been practicing." She gave him a cheeky glare and then sighed. "They're not used to my doing anything so out of character. I never *have* done anything out of character. But I thought maybe, since I'm thirty-two now..." She shrugged, exasperated all over again, and Matthew finished the thought for her.

"You thought that if you told them how you felt, they'd be able to support you?"

"I know who they are. I know what they can and can't handle. I've never expected more from them than they could give, but after last night when you and I talked, I hoped for more." She shrugged and gazed up at the ceiling. "Being with them tonight, I felt lonelier than I have in my whole life." She rolled her head to look at him. "Does that sound weird?"

"No." He brushed her cheek with his knuckles. "Not to me."

Tracing her cheekbone with his thumb, Matthew said, "I think we expect more than the people we love can give. We expect—" he shook his head sadly "—something different." Turning to her more fully, he searched her eyes. "If it turns out that they can't support you in this, will you change your mind?"

She didn't even have to think about it. "No." Never before had she felt so sure about anything...or so certain she was right. "I'm not going to change my mind."

"Good." Respect and something else—a deep satisfaction—filled his gaze.

"But I can't imagine raising my child without even one set of grandparents. I can't give her a father, and now I may not be able to give her grandparents, either."

Without warning, Emily's eyes filled with tears. Conviction yielded to sorrow in a heartbeat.

Matthew pulled her into his arms without a second thought. One hand cupped her head, the other rested on her back. Tears rolled down her cheeks as he rocked her.

"You'll give her your love." Matthew whispered the words against her temple. "You'll give her your gentleness and your strength." His tone brooked no doubt. "You'll be so good at it, Em."

He kissed her temple and her forehead. Emily clung to him, letting his confidence envelope her. She stayed where she was until her tears dried.

"Thank you," she murmured against his neck.

Matthew smiled into her hair. He pulled back, framing her face with his hands. Kissing her gently for comfort, he brushed back her hair. Emily stared as if hypnotized, and slowly, cautiously, Matthew lowered his head again.

It happened as if in slow motion.

Rising like smoke, Emily's arms curled around his neck. Her lips parted and she arched forward, heedless of Matthew's careful restraint. What started as his idea soon became hers as Emily Gardiner gave Matthew Carter the kiss she had been saving for more than half of her life.

And nothing in her whole, circumspect life had ever felt so good. Or so right.

Chapter Six

To Matthew, Emily's kiss felt like rain in August: it nurtured; it restored; it offered solace; it gave relief.

The inexperience of her touch was clear, but he perceived immediately the beauty inherent in the innocence. Her lips were guileless.

For a moment, his mouth did not move beneath hers. Then, from deep within him, came the desire to respond. The urge to part his lips, to draw her inside, seemed to burgeon from mild to overwhelming in an instant. And in that instant, he withdrew from the need. He pulled back from Emily as though her lips were on fire.

His abrupt move made Emily's eyelids pop open. Her vision was hazy and out of focus. When it cleared she saw Matthew standing by the couch. He was staring at her, his expression wary.

The two friends had no words for each other, no way to diffuse the awkwardness of the moment.

Dear Lord, what have I done? Emily thought.

And he stood motionless, wondering, *What's the matter with me? She's my friend.*

They continued to stare at each other, Matthew locked in shock at his reaction, Emily locked in dismay at her temerity.

The moment her lips had touched his, nearly twenty years of wondering and longing and imagining had turned comforting into soul shattering.

Matthew's experience had been just as explosive. She had given him the sweetest, most chaste kiss he had ever received, and he had responded to it with a gut-wrenching thirst for more.

He looked at Emily now—at the long russet hair and creamy, fair skin that seemed to beckon him to another time, a gentler time he'd left behind years ago. Her lips were slightly parted and her brows were drawn together. She looked so sweetly confused and so hurt.

Raking a hand through his hair, Matthew took a deep breath to steady himself.

Damning the fact that he'd pulled away so abruptly, he shook his head at her, a small, regretful smile on his lips.

"I'm sorry, Em."

Emily heard the word as if it echoed throughout her living room. She had kissed him, and he was *sorry*.

She stood, forcing a smile that was as nonchalant as she could muster. "Don't be sorry." She shrugged. "I just wanted to say thank you. I should have kissed your cheek."

"It's my fault." Matthew smiled sadly. "I'm a little rusty at relationships."

He backed out of the space between the sofa and coffee table. Polite to the end, Emily followed him to the front door.

With his hand on the knob, Matthew turned back to her. "If you're not doing anything tomorrow night, I'd like you to come to Carter House, see what I'm planning to do to the place." He shrugged. "I could use some advice."

Emily shrugged back. "Okay." Her voice was as casual as his, her expression as uncertain.

There were no other words as Matthew opened her door and walked out into the night.

Twenty minutes after leaving Emily's cottage, Matthew stood in the master bedroom of Carter House with a razor in his hand and a can of shaving cream balanced on the pedestal sink.

Like everything else in the house his uncle Fisher had willed to him, the mirror in the master bedroom was older than Matthew himself—a lot older. The two-story, three-bedroom house dated back to the early 1920s and most of the fixtures were the original pieces. The beveled mirror was pitted in some places, chipped in others, and there was a long crack running diagonally from the top right corner to the bottom left. It divided Matthew's reflection into two unequal parts.

That, he thought wryly, looking at the jagged image of his head, *seems fitting.*

Matthew did not view his life as a fluid whole. Rather, he saw his past as something divided into separate parts, one piece having little to do with another.

The part he was thinking about now was the distant past, a time that seemed to belong to another man, another life, another plane altogether.

"You sure as hell don't *look* the same," he told the reflection.

For the past year and a half, he experienced a perverse satisfaction every time he looked into a mirror to glimpse his hair long and unstyled, his face shadowed by a coarse beard.

It had been years since he'd felt any connection to the young man he had been. Still, he had kept up the charade, wearing the trappings of his success like a costume to cover the dissatisfaction in his soul.

During the past year, it had pleased him to drop the mask, to let his appearance reflect his anger and his unwillingness to please anyone but himself.

But each time he saw Emily, something inside him softened. He had no explanation for his reaction to her tonight and no explanation for what he was about to do, except that he felt the moustache and beard were no longer necessary.

Shaking the can of shaving cream, Matthew squirted a good amount into his palm, spread the foam over his cheeks and chin, and started shaving. And as he shaved, he remembered....

"Oh, McCarthy were dead and McKinney didn't know it and McKinney were dead and McCarthy didn't know it, and they both lay dead in the very same bed, and neither knew that the other were dead!"

With a hearty abandon—and a voice more used to shouting than singing—Matthew belted the song his uncle Fisher had taught him the day before. He waded out to the deepest part of the creek as he sang, then punched up the volume on the chorus as he spread his fingers across his chest, checking for hairs. He found none, as usual, but he wasn't too disappointed; at twelve, there was still time.

Certain he was alone, Matthew leisurely inspected his biceps, flexing the muscle to see if it had grown since yesterday.

"Oh, McCarthy were dead!" he sang, twisting his torso with his arms in the air.

When a splash resounded behind him, Matthew dropped his hands and spun around, accidentally letting loose his mother's least favorite word.

Water flew near the bank opposite him. Two pale arms flailed and a head covered with wet, red hair stuck up just above the water.

With giant strides, Matthew moved to the madly splashing person. Reaching below the water, he felt for armpits, found them and lifted.

Up popped a redheaded girl, younger than he and fully clothed. Her long hair was sopping wet from her ears to her waist. She snorted water and wiped her face with her hands.

"What happened?" Matthew barked. "Did you fall in?"

She stood in the water with her back to him, and when he tried to turn her around, she resisted.

"Are you hurt anywhere?"

Wordlessly, she shook her head.

Matthew put a hand on her shoulder. She jerked away and without further ado, or even a thank-you, she scrambled onto the bank.

Frowning, his hands on his hips, Matthew watched her go until he realized she was limping.

"Hey! Wait a minute!" he called as he climbed onto the bank after her.

The girl sped up and her limp became more pronounced.

"Hold on!" he hollered.

"I c-can't. I—I have to get home," she called in a high voice, without so much as glancing over her shoulder. "I'll be late for dinner."

He caught up with her in a few easy strides, grabbing her arm as gently as he could and holding her still.

"I just want to see where you're hurt," he told her.

"I'm not hurt." Her voice was thin and strained and oddly squeaky, even for a girl, Matthew thought.

She did not look at him. She looked at the sky, at the trees; she searched the space above her head. She looked everywhere but at him.

"Are you in shock or something?" Matthew looked her over and frowned.

She was skinny and pale. She wore blue jeans and a blue shirt with flowers on the collar. Her clothes were plastered to her and Matthew had the urge to pick her up and wring her out. Even wet, her hair was the reddest he'd ever seen.

"Hey, I know who you are. You're Jessica Gardiner's cousin, aren't you? What's your name?"

"Emily."

Matthew nodded. "Jessica's in my class. How'd you fall in the creek?"

"I lost my footing," Emily answered, still without meeting his gaze.

Matthew tightened his hold on her arm. "Come on, I'd better take you home."

"No!" Emily yanked free of his hold. "You'd better go...go back into the water!" She made shooing motions with her hands, keeping not only her eyes, but her whole head averted as far as her neck would allow.

"What's the matter with you?" Matthew demanded, leaning left in an effort to see her face. "Did you hit your head on a rock or something when you fell in?"

He took her arm again, and between Emily's attempts to escape and his attempts to calm her down, she wound up facing him dead on.

She squeezed her eyes shut tight.

Matthew shook his head. Shock or no shock, he was about to let her find her own way home, when finally, almost as if she couldn't help herself, she inched one eyelid open.

Her single-eyed gaze swept down his torso. At the lowest point of her perusal, her other eye popped open, as well.

"You're wearing swimming trunks!" she breathed. Relief, followed swiftly by disappointment, flashed across her small face.

Matthew stared at her. "You're weird."

"I thought—" She stopped abruptly, her cheeks aflame.

"You thought what?"

"I've got to go home. I'm late." Emily turned and started off again.

She made it only a few steps before Matthew caught her from behind. Lifting her up, he flipped her over so that she was hanging upside down.

"You thought what?" He bounced her up and down. "Tell me!"

"Let me go! Put me down!"

"Tell me!" Matthew demanded again. "Tell me or else!"

His face lathered with shaving cream, Matthew grinned at the memory of his first encounter with Emily. What he'd finally bounced out of her that day was that she had overheard her cousin Jessica telling a friend that boys waded *naked* in Willow Kiss creek. Emily had wanted to see for herself, but the bank had been muddy, and her spying had landed her smack in the water.

He still remembered his solemn promise not to tell her parents what she had been up to. He and Emily had been friends from that moment on.

Even as a kid he had viewed her company as a respite from the rest of his life, a comfortable haven.

Lifting his chin, Matthew shaved below his jaw. He tapped the razor against the sink, turned on the faucet and watched water and shaving cream swirl together in the porcelain basin. Grabbing a washcloth, he wiped the residual shaving cream from his face.

His response to Emily tonight wasn't all that confusing, he decided. She was, after all, everything he'd been missing for years: the sweetness, the warmth, the honesty. But loneliness and need were not reason enough to take a relationship from friendship to romance, assuming Emily was willing.

Leaning toward the mirror, he studied his face clean-shaven. He looked more like the old Matthew Carter on the outside, but inside? He shook his head. Inside, he was who he was. A kiss could not change a man. In his experience, no one person could heal another. And the man he had become would be lousy relationship material.

Bending down over the sink, he splashed cold water on his face, reached for a clean towel and straightened up.

A friend, he could try to be. But a husband, a lover, a father? No. Never again.

Chapter Seven

"Excuse me, miss, do you know who wrote *A Midsummer Night's Dream?*"

On her knees in the picture-book section, Emily pushed *The Dream Weaver* into its proper place and straightened up. She'd been shelving books on and off for two hours. Now, an hour away from closing, her hip and back were killing her.

"William Shakespeare," she answered without looking up. "You'll find him in the drama section."

"Oh, good. What does he look like?"

Emily sat back on her heels. "What does he look— Aunt Tillie!" she exclaimed, shaking her head as the elderly woman giggled delightedly.

"You didn't even know it was me! I lowered my voice," Tillie confided, her bright little eyes twinkling. "Lilly always says there's more humor in a day at the library than in a month of TV."

Emily nodded. "Mmm. Where *is* Aunt Lilly?"

Tillie glanced toward the back of the library. "She's wiping down the sink in the women's room. You know how she is. Hurry, Emily, get up. I want to talk to you before she comes out."

Emily struggled to her feet. Her aunt looked nervous and a little excited. "What's up?"

"Oh, Emily, I couldn't wait to talk to you. I felt so awful yesterday, not telling you how I felt about your announcement. But, you know, Lil and I live in your parents' home, and they wouldn't have understood our contradicting them." She threaded her thin fingers together. "Dear, I think what you're doing is wonderful. Don't you let *anyone* talk you out of it."

Tillie's sweet face was earnest and intent. Emily looked at the elderly woman in wonder. "You'd really support my having a baby on my own?"

"Yes, I would." Tillie's mouth firmed stubbornly. "Every woman should have that option. There was a time when I wanted to be a mother myself."

Emily's eyes widened. "I never knew that."

Tillie nodded. "That's what I wanted to talk to you about before Lilly returns."

Her sharp blue eyes darted around the children's book section to ensure that they were relatively alone. Her voice dropped to a whisper. "I had a beau once. We were very much in love."

"Aunt Tillie, you were in love?" Emily huddled next to her aunt. "When? Who was he?"

Tillie giggled again. "You're so surprised. I knew you would be."

"And Aunt Lilly doesn't know?"

"She knows. She was in love with someone, too, but she doesn't like to talk about it." She sobered slightly. "Everyone in the family thinks your Aunt Lilly and I were destined to be spinsters from the day we were born. But we have our secrets, Emily. I won't tell you who my love was, because that's my memory to cherish. But I will tell you that it was wonderful. I think every woman should follow her heart. We all need someone special to love. And a child in this family would be wonderful. Maybe you'll have twins! My grandmother Risa and her brother were twins."

Emily looked shocked. "I never thought of that. Oh my."

Tillie laughed. "Here comes your aunt." She raised her voice as Lil approached. "Well, how does the sink look?"

"Fine now." Lilly strode into the children's section with a verve that belied her advanced years.

"If each person would simply take a paper towel, fold it—" she mimed folding the towel "—and wipe down the faucet and the basin, the bathroom would stay fresh for the next patron's use, but no—"

"Lilly, please. We're all very familiar with your views on lavatory sanitation." Tillie leaned toward Emily and confided, "Back in forty-seven, your aunt wanted to put a coin box on the bathroom door and *charge* people to get in!"

"Yes," Lilly confirmed. "Because people appreciate what they pay for!"

Her sister shrugged. "I told Emily how we feel about the baby."

Lil's expression brightened at the mention of her potential great-great-niece or nephew.

She smiled. "Good. So you know we're for it. I'm ashamed that we didn't say anything to you last night."

Emily was amazed to see Lilly's high cheekbones flush pink. Lil had always seemed too gruff to embarrass easily.

Their show of solidarity touched and pleased her.

"You have nothing to be ashamed of." Emily touched Lilly's bony knuckles where they bulged from gripping her handbag. "I feel one hundred percent better already. My child is going to have two wonderful role models."

Her aunts beamed.

"Well, this is certainly a pleasant surprise. My three favorite librarians all together in the finest library this side of Boston."

"Matthew Carter!"

The twins grinned hugely as Matthew walked up between them and gave them each a warm squeeze. Both women spoke at once, exclaiming their pleasure at seeing him again and insisting that he hadn't changed at all except to get more handsome.

Emily had to agree.

Clean-shaven, Matthew looked very much like he had on his wedding day. *He's still the handsomest man I've ever seen,* she thought, marveling that in all these years—and after last night—her reaction upon seeing him remained the same: her pulse speeded up and her thinking slowed down.

Giving herself a mental shake, she smiled. "Excuse me. I'll let the three of you become reacquainted while I finish up."

"Wait." Matthew reached out a hand to stop her. "I know you're busy, but I have a question for you."

"That's what I'm here for. What would you like to know?"

Matthew rubbed the place where his moustache used to be. "It doesn't have to do with books, I'm afraid."

If her businesslike demeanor was meant to throw him off balance, it worked. Matthew began to feel, of all things, shy! Self-consciously, he rubbed a finger across his bare upper lip. Emily was wearing a light green dress with a scoop neck. The material fell straight to her hips and then flared softly into a swirling skirt.

He liked it. He liked it, he thought, too damn much.

He remembered teasing her about her red curls when they were kids, but he had no desire to tease her today. Her hair was lovely—soft and lush and the color of maple leaves in autumn. Her skin was smooth and pale as cream, and her eyes were the muted green of Willow Kiss in the summer. Last night, he had determined definitively that they would be friends and nothing more. Today, he knew that he was seeing Emily, the woman, for the very first time.

He realized that he was staring when she prompted him, "What do you want to ask me?"

"Oh." He frowned. He had intended to ask if she was still coming to his house this evening, but now, maddeningly, he felt like a teenager trying to muster the courage to ask for a first date.

"I...uh..." He scowled. "Do you have any books on remodeling?"

Shoving his hands into the pockets of his jeans, he followed Emily to the appropriate section, answered her questions about the type of remodeling he intended to do and waited while she made the selections. She gave him a new library card and checked out his books. He thanked her, still without asking whether she was coming to his house that evening.

Stalling, he took his books to a table and leafed through them without seeing anything. Emily's aunts sat down to talk to him, and finally, five minutes before closing, Matthew asked them if they would like to come to Carter House to see his remodeling plans.

"Oh, yes, that would be a such a treat!" Tillie responded with an enthusiasm that made him smile. "I love that wonderful old place. I remember the first day Fisher opened it as a boarding house. Lilly and I had just started working at the library. It was that long ago, but I can see it as if it were yesterday. Fisher put up that plaque—"

"Room and Board for Residents, Visitors and Passersby," Lil supplied, nodding.

"He got his first boarder that very afternoon. Oh, how excited he was!"

"He had a gift for making people feel welcome," Lilly stated.

"He treated everyone who stayed there like family." Tillie agreed with her sister, and the twins fell into silent but happy reminiscence.

Leaving the sisters to their memories, Matthew went to find Emily at the front desk. She was checking out the last books of the day, and he waited impatiently for the final patron to leave.

Emily smiled blandly as he approached the desk. She tapped a stack of index cards together to align their edges.

Matthew spoke without preamble. "Are you still coming to see the house tonight? Your aunts are going to come over."

"They are?" Emily glanced at her aunts. They were speaking in whispers even though library hours were officially over. Lilly had risen and was lining up the spines in the new-releases section. "They always loved Carter House," Emily murmured.

"How about you?" Matthew asked her. "Did you love it, too?"

She met his eyes. "Yes, I loved it. Who wouldn't?"

"Most of my father's family, for starters." He smiled wryly. "They thought Fisher was crazy. He embarrassed them."

Emily shook her head. "He wasn't crazy. He was . . . beyond the pale."

Matthew grinned. "There's a description he would have liked."

Fisher Carter had made his boarding house a welcoming haven for wandering eccentrics. Solitary people had come together in his home to create their own family, of sorts. And the denizens of Carter House had loved having young people around. They had doted on Matthew and his friends.

"I miss your uncle Fisher," Emily told him softly.

"Yeah, me too."

"And you know something? I miss Carter House the way it was, too. You threw some wonderful parties in that big old basement."

Matthew laughed. "I always felt that the rest of the house belonged to Fisher, but the basement was mine."

"Are you going to finish the basement?"

"I know I'm going to dry-wall. Beyond that, I could use a little advice."

The only person to whom Emily had ever given domestic advice was herself. She had virtually given up the dream of picking out wallpaper and furniture with anyone other than her mother. How could she resist helping Matthew decide whether a wall should be papered or painted? It might be the closest she'd ever come to "picking out a pattern."

"I still have a little work to finish up here. We could be over in an hour or so, if that's all right."

"I'll wait."

"It's going to take me at least a half hour. Why don't you—"

"I'll wait."

Matthew walked over to the table where Tillie was rereading *Forever Amber*. He opened one of the remodeling books and soon he and the twins were heavily involved in a discussion of pedestal sinks versus cabinet-style.

Emily decided that if she wanted to maintain her sanity, she would finish her work and get through this evening as quickly as possible.

Matthew at her dining room table...Matthew on the couch in her living room...Matthew seated at one of the long wooden tables in her library—she was making enough memories to torture herself for a lifetime.

What, she wondered, was he going to do with Carter House when he finished the repairs? She would ask him this evening. If he was intent on selling immediately, that information would be a good reminder that they were at cross-purposes in their lives, because now she, too, had an agenda.

A funny, tickling nervousness fluttered in her stomach. By this time next week, she would have taken the first step on her own path to a new life. At 3:00 p.m. next Tuesday, she was going to have her first consultation with the doctor who was going to help her conceive a child.

"What color will you paint it, Matthew?" Lil asked, her eyes on the wall of the master bedroom.

While her sister appraised the walls, Tillie gave the ceiling moldings her attention. The master bedroom of Carter House had captured the twins's interest.

"I don't think it should be painted at all," Tillie decided. "Wallpaper—that's what this room calls for. It's simply crying out for sunshine-yellow paper with a vine-and-flower pattern."

"Sunshine-yellow paper!" Lil screwed up her features. "I don't like to contradict you, Tillie, but if this room is crying out for anything, it's paint. Robin's-egg-blue paint."

Tillie shook her snowy head and smiled. "Paper, Lilly dear. It's simply begging for it."

"Tillie—" Lil moved to stand toe-to-toe with her sister "—I'm a little surprised by your stubbornness, because these walls are practically screaming, 'Paint me.'"

"*Wallpaper* me."

"*Paint* me!"

"Wallpaper me, Lilly Rose!"

"Paint me, Tillie Lucille!"

Emily nudged Matthew with her elbow.

On the verge of intervening before the elderly sisters came to fisticuffs, Matthew glanced down at Emily. She motioned to the hallway, nodding firmly when Matthew wavered.

In the hall, she sagged against the wall and sighed. "Trust me," she said, "I've seen them do this a hundred times—never over someone else's decorating scheme, of course. You just have to let them duke it out.''

Grinning, Matthew shook his head. "No wonder we always returned our library books on time." He rubbed a hand over his chin and slanted a look at her. "You haven't noticed my new face."

Emily smiled. "Yes, I have. It looks very nice."

"Think so?" He grinned more broadly.

Guiding Emily by the elbow, Matthew led her downstairs. "So, you think I should leave the window seat in the dining room?"

They walked into the large, formal dining area, where Emily reaffirmed her earlier opinion. "I love window seats. I have no idea why they put one in the dining room, but I'd keep it."

"I wonder who 'they' were?" Matthew mused. "To my knowledge, there was only one family in here before Fisher bought the place, but I have no idea who they were."

"In a town like this, it probably wouldn't be that hard to find out." Emily walked to a sideboard that was built into the wall. She smoothed a palm over the finished mahogany. "I'll always think of this house as Fisher's, though, no matter who owned it before."

"Will you think of it as Fisher's once I've painted it robin's-egg blue?"

"Or wallpapered it sunshine yellow?" Emily grinned, turning toward him. It seemed like a good time to ask the question that was nagging her. "Are you planning to hang on to the house?"

The hardwood creaked cozily as he walked to the window. He brushed dust off the pane with his forefinger. "I like the old place. But it wouldn't be financially feasible to hang on to it if I'm not living in it or using it as income property."

He looked over his shoulder and smiled. "I don't want to be an absentee landlord, and I can't really see myself running a boarding house."

Emily returned his smile, but the news that he had no intention of settling in True left her feeling deflated. "I hope you sell it to a big family," she said. "I remember how noisy dinners could be in this room. I loved that."

Matthew nodded. His parents used to complain about "Fisher's misfits," and it hurt Matthew now to recall that he, too, had been embarrassed at times by his uncle's life-style and friends.

"You know, I think that half the time, Fisher never even collected rent for the rooms." Matthew turned toward Emily fully and sat on the window bench. "What are you doing for dinner?"

"Dinner?" Emily frowned. "Well, I think my aunts have already eaten." She checked her watch. "It's after seven. It was almost five-thirty when they got to the library, and you know how older people are. They like to eat early."

"How about younger people? You haven't had dinner yet. I heard your stomach growl when we were in the basement."

Emily stalled. She walked the perimeter of the large dining room as though dinner with him was a decision that required careful deliberation.

Matthew watched her in some amusement. She was wearing low shoes, which he assumed were easy on her back. On the heels of that practical realization came the observation that she had beautiful calves. They were slender and shapely and long. With every step she took, her flowing skirt seemed to flirt with her legs.

And with him.

Dragging his attention off her body and onto her face—which didn't settle him one iota—Matthew stood, but stayed near the window, on the opposite side of the room.

He attempted a grin in an effort to leaven his own feelings. "I like noisy dining rooms, too, Emily. Why don't you take pity on me? We can go to Calamity Jane's. I've been wondering if they still have the best chili north of Texas."

"They do. But I brought a lot of work home with me. I'm taking two days off next week, and I want everything to be caught up at the library."

Matthew's grin slowly disappeared. Before he could try to change her mind, Tillie and Lilly came arguing down the stairs.

"You've been color-blind since 1942!" Lilly spat disgustedly, pushing roughly past her sister to enter the dining room. Although there was plenty of room, Tillie made a point of bumping Lilly aside on *her* way into the room.

Emily winced. The way the twins deliberately shoved into each other during arguments, it was a wonder they hadn't broken bones long ago. Family lore had it that the only reason they wore rubber-soled shoes was to gain traction during arguments.

"Are you ready to leave?" Emily checked her watch, hoping to stave off another invitation to dinner. Since she was trying to cut down on self-inflicted torments, dinner with Matthew was strictly off-limits.

"Oh, gosh," she told her aunts, "if we don't hurry, you're going to miss *Jeopardy!*"

"So what?" Tillie said dismissively with a wave of her hand as she went to take a last look at the sideboard. "Why should Alex Trebek have all the fun?"

"That's right," Lil seconded, smoothly shifting gears to agree with her twin. "Watching people live it up on TV while we sit home every night with Rose and Ernest is no picnic, let me tell you. A deader couple of doorknobs you'll never find."

"No offense to your parents, Emily dear." Tillie smiled sweetly.

"Have you ladies eaten?" Matthew interjected smoothly. "I was just asking Emily if she wanted to go over to Calamity Jane's."

To her credit, Emily knew when she was licked. Her aunts' eyes lit like sparklers on the Fourth of July.

"Best corn bread you'll ever eat," Lilly stated enthusiastically, smiling the broad, close-lipped smile she reserved for true excitement.

"And they make the most delicious strawberry-rhubarb pie!" Tillie was already on her way to the front door. "We hardly ever go there anymore. It's not wise to eat out too frequently when you're on a fixed income."

"Tillie!" Lil shot her sister a reproving glare.

"Oh." Tillie put two fingers to her lips. She looked at Emily apologetically. "I didn't mean to complain. We do very well on what we've saved and with what we get from the government."

"If you two ever need anything, I hope you'll ask me or ask Mother and Father." Emily frowned. A little fist of shame tightened inside her chest. Before today, she hadn't guessed that her aunts were anything but content with their lives.

Tillie smiled gratefully. "We're fine, dear," she said again, then twinkled up at Matthew. "But strawberry-rhubarb pie would be a welcome treat."

"With pleasure, Tillie." Matthew opened the front door, holding it solicitously while the other women passed through.

Emily followed immediately after her aunts, but Matthew stopped her, holding her elbow while the twins bustled down the front walk.

Even at five foot six, Emily felt enveloped by Matthew's presence. He was half a foot taller and many inches wider than she, and he was holding her closely enough to speak without being heard by the ladies out front.

"You still don't want to go. Why not?"

Because a low voice and broad shoulders are a lethal combination for a maiden librarian with the biggest crush in world history, Emily admitted to herself, unable to utter even the most innocuous excuse when her face was this close to his chest. She could feel the warmth of his body and smell the masculine scent that seemed to comfort and exhilarate her at the same time.

What if the rooms behind them were filled with furniture? What if this were *their* house?

She pursed her lips. Those were exactly the questions she didn't want to ask herself. Summoning a weak smile, she answered, "I do want to go, but it's getting late."

Matthew tossed his head back. "Ahh, that's the problem. You have a curfew." He grinned. "I promise not to keep you out past it."

Amused despite herself, Emily pulled her elbow out of his grasp and scowled deliberately. "Your *boyish* charm has convinced me, Mr. Carter."

"Boyish!" Matthew placed a hand over his heart. "I'm wounded."

Gesturing for her to pass ahead of him, Matthew followed her out the door. She was making her way carefully down the porch steps when he spoke behind her.

"I bet *you* don't get many overdue books, either, Miss Emily."

She didn't have to turn around to know that he was grinning.

Chapter Eight

They took Emily's car to Calamity Jane's.

When they were settled in a booth, with bowls of chili, crusty, golden slabs of corn bread, and huge, juicy slices of rhubarb pie covering the table, Matthew asked Emily about the two days she planned to take off from work the following week.

"Is this a mini-vacation you're talking about?"

"No." Tearing open a small packet of honey, she squeezed half into her tea and the other half over a slice of corn bread.

Emily debated skirting the reason for her time off. Every person at this table supported her decision to have a baby, but it was a good bet that in the history of their small town, no one had conceived a child via the method she was going to use. She had to keep reminding herself that alternative insemination was exactly that—an alternative, not some bizarre scientific experiment.

She took a sip of her tea and looked at their curious faces. "I'm going to Portland to see the doctor who's going to help me have a baby."

Emily's aunts were delighted. No thrill could compare to the prospect of becoming great-great-aunts. Matthew, however, showed an increased interest in his chili. He stirred it, frowned, stirred some more.

Finally, he dropped his spoon and raised his eyes. "So soon?"

"Soon?" Emily laughed. "I've been thinking about this for over a year."

Lips pressed into a firm line, Matthew reached for a packet of soda crackers. He crushed them between his fingers, ripped open the cellophane and poured the cracker pieces onto his chili. Emily had seen him do that very thing a dozen or more times in their youth, usually at this restaurant. He leaned against the back of the booth and leveled his blue gaze at her.

"Is this an appointment for a consultation or to begin the procedure?"

"It's for a physical and a consultation." She spoke in a low voice and glanced pointedly around the room. "Maybe we shouldn't discuss this right now."

Matthew ignored her. "Where is this doctor?"

"I told you, in Portland."

"Hmm." He sliced off a hunk of corn bread, buttered it and left it untouched on his plate. He radiated tension.

Emily's aunts were watching him with wide, interested eyes.

"You've examined all of this thoroughly from a legal standpoint, I presume? Rights of the father, for example, if it should ever come to that?"

"You didn't ask me any of this a day ago." She looked at him suspiciously. "I thought you supported me in this."

"I do." A waitress came by with coffee, and Matthew held out his cup. "Thank you," he murmured, his eyes still locked with Emily's. "Not knowing who the father is could complicate matters from a legal standpoint, that's all I'm saying."

"You believe Emily will run into problems?" Tillie asked with concern.

"On the contrary," Emily spoke up firmly, "not having a man involved should make it *less* complicated."

Matthew set his coffee cup solidly on the table. "A man will be involved, Emily, you just won't know who he is."

Emily darted a quick glance at her aunts and a prolonged glare at her "friend." He was worrying her family needlessly and, almost worse, he was making her feel that she was once again completely without support.

With ladylike precision, she pushed the heavy ceramic bowl of chili away and placed the brown mug of tea on the paper placemat in front of her. She looked at Matthew pointedly.

"I don't mind not knowing the biological father's identity." She smiled. "You know what they say—men should be seen and not heard."

"*Children* should be seen and not heard," Matthew corrected.

Emily raised an eloquent brow.

Lil and Tillie exchanged shocked but vastly amused glances and leaned forward with their hands braced on the edge of the table to enjoy the rest of the show, looking more like twins than they ever had before. The sisters were seated in the center of the booth, with Matthew and Emily across from each other on the ends. Matthew leaned toward her as far as he could without putting his chest in the chili.

"A few days ago you minded not knowing who the father will be," he reminded her, his voice and expression dripping with innuendo.

Emily darted a furious, telling look in her aunts' direction and shook her head at Matthew.

"Oh, don't mind us, Emily," Tillie reassured eagerly. "We aren't listening."

"I want you two to know that I have thought this through—every aspect of it—very carefully. I have done a good deal of research and I've chosen a clinic that has performed this procedure many times before." She looked at Matthew. "And there has never been any legal fallout regarding the donor. I asked." Emily smiled at her aunts. "Your support means more to me than I can say. I hope you'll continue to lend it."

Amid their swift and adamant reassurance, Matthew felt like the fourth wheel of a tricycle.

Frowning, he picked up his spoon and knocked a kidney bean under the surface of his chili. Hell, he was just trying to be practical. He wanted to protect Emily....

But from what?

She looked frail, he realized, but she wasn't. She spoke to her aunts with confidence and with the grace and poise that was as much a part of her as that curling red hair.

Her appearance was deceptive: the translucent skin, the delicate features, her slender body. She was going to look so beautiful when she was pregnant. Beautiful and delicate and strong.

He became aware of the conversation again as Lil questioned Emily about the doctor.

"Will you stay in the hospital overnight for the tests or are you going to be in a hotel?"

"A motel, actually, I think. Probably one outside the city. I'd like to save a little money."

Tillie reached over and touched Emily's hand. "You're going to think I'm a worrywart, I know, but I wish you weren't going alone. Portland isn't as safe as it used to be."

Lilly nodded in agreement.

"I'll lock my car doors and find a very safe motel," Emily assured them. "I'd ask you to come with me so we could do the town, but I need you to take over at the library while I'm gone."

Lilly, especially, was clearly excited by the prospect of working again. The sisters had covered for Emily before on the rare occasions when she was forced to miss a day.

"Still," Tillie persisted, "going through this by yourself? Lilly and I always go to the doctor together. It's much more comforting. Maybe you could ask a friend."

"She already has." Matthew's deep-voiced pronouncement surprised all three women.

"I never asked you to come with me," Emily denied.

"You asked for my support." *And for a damn sight more than that,* he reminded her with a quelling look as he prepared for an argument.

He had made up his mind. He wasn't going to let her go through this alone, because the bottom line was that no matter how capable she seemed, she was still a small-town woman with small-town experiences. She had a trusting nature that would make her easy prey for people more streetwise than she, and almost anyone he could think of was more streetwise than Emily.

Certainly the doctor who was going to make money off a single woman's desire to have a child was more streetwise, Matthew decided cynically. The men who were willing to become fathers in a biological sense only were more streetwise. And aside from all that, Portland was a hundred and fifty miles away and Emily's car was not in the greatest condition. Had she even checked her oil recently?

"I'm going," he said with as much force as if she had been arguing with him for hours.

Emily hadn't said a word, of course, and she chose not to reply now. She watched him warily, showing neither gratitude nor relief nor irritation.

Matthew shifted uncomfortably on the maroon vinyl of the booth, took a bite of cold chili and soggy crackers and swallowed with effort.

He took a sip of black coffee and smiled ingenuously at the three bemused women. "That's what friends are for."

"Cookie?" Emily tipped the box of chocolate-chip cookies in Matthew's direction.

"No, thank you." He pushed his aviator-style sunglasses further up the bridge of his nose.

"Popcorn? Jelly beans?" Emily sorted through the large paper bag of snacks she'd brought along for the trip. "I have fat-free fig bars and rippled potato chips.

Oh, would you like a stalk of celery? I stuffed it with cream cheese and pimentos. Or—''

"Emily, for crying out loud, this is a two-and-a-half-hour car ride. You've been offering me food for the last thirty minutes, and we haven't even left the county yet!''

"Sorry,'' Emily murmured, shoving junk food back into the sack. She readjusted her seat belt, sat back and folded her hands in her lap. "I'm a little nervous.''

An understatement if ever there was one, she thought. For the past week, she hadn't known where to focus her concern: on the purpose of the trip she was about to make or on the fact that Matthew was coming with her. She had tried to dissuade him from joining her in every way possible, short of telling him flat out that he was not welcome.

She needed to focus positively on the process of alternative insemination. With Matthew by her side, it was too easy to imagine having the baby the "usual'' way—with someone she loved. With him along, it was too easy to start fretting over the fact that she would never know the father of her child.

For the past couple of days, she had stayed as far away from him as she could, which hadn't been too difficult, she reflected gloomily. As far as she knew, Matthew hadn't left Carter House.

Busy with her thoughts, she almost jumped when his hand covered her twined fingers.

His palm was warm and slightly rough. *From working with his wood and on the house, no doubt.* She looked up at him when he gave her hands a little squeeze.

"I'm nervous, too,'' he said.

"You're nervous? Why are *you* nervous?"

His sunglasses were the dark, impenetrable kind that shaded his expression as well as his eyes, but his lips twitched with a reluctant smile.

"It's not every day that I take a girl to Portland to get her pregnant."

Emily gaped at him, unsure of whether to laugh or lecture him on the merits of decorous speech. She was about to pull her hand from his, when she realized that his palm was perspiring.

He *was* nervous!

Rather than increasing her misgivings, Matthew's show of nerves calmed her. She smiled gently. "This trip is just for the initial consultation. They're not going to do anything, except take some tests and maybe give me some instructions to follow."

Matthew nodded. He considered making a joke about being a nervous father, but thought better of it. Keeping his eyes on the road, he drove without speaking.

Emily tuned the radio in to an oldies station and sat back. Five minutes passed. Her nervousness returned.

I'm just jittery because I'm going to see a doctor, she told herself stolidly, adding the affirmation, *I know I am making the right decision for my life.* She took a relaxing breath and sighed, then reached forward for her bag of snacks.

She opened the paper sack as quietly as she could, trying not to draw Matthew's attention to the fact that she was, once again, rummaging through the food. Binging was not, after all, the mark of a confident, relaxed woman.

Carefully, she withdrew the package of chocolate-chip cookies. Every rustle of paper, every crackle of cellophane reverberated through the interior of the automobile as though it were an announcement being broadcast over a public address system: *"Your attention, please. Nervous woman in car."*

Extracting a cookie, she nibbled daintily, then almost bolted out of her seat when Matthew reached into the package she had placed on her lap. Like startled birds, her hands flew away from the cellophane as he fumbled with the wrapping.

They spent the rest of the trip eating the crackers and cookies that Emily set on the bench between them.

"Which exit do I take?" Matthew asked when they reached the Portland city limits.

Emily checked the directions she'd placed on the dashboard. "Broadway."

Matthew glanced at his watch. "I allowed enough time for us to have lunch before your appointment." He slid her a glance. "Any chance you're still hungry?"

Grimacing, Emily pressed a hand to her stomach. "If I look at anything that even remotely resembles food, I may be ill. If you'd like to stop somewhere, though, I can always get a cup of tea."

"Or a stomach pump." Matthew laughed for the first time that morning. "I think I've done enough damage, too." He watched for the off ramp, then followed Emily's directions.

They were a few blocks from the clinic when Matthew cleared his throat. "Thank you for letting me come with you today, Em."

Emily looked at him and nodded. Thoughtfully, she rubbed her finger over a loose thread in her skirt. "Why did you want to?"

Flexing his fingers on the steering wheel, Matthew shrugged. "I felt alone when I came back here." He turned to her. "You changed that. And I didn't want you to be alone today."

Emily's face flushed with pleasure. "I'm glad you came," she told him, and realized that she meant it.

When they arrived at their destination, Matthew parked the car and escorted Emily through the clinic's wide glass doors. The reception area was decorated attractively in soothing shades of mauve and pale, pearly pink. Framed prints of impressionist gardens hung on the wall. Over the sofa, there was a print of a mother and child by the artist Mary Cassatt.

The reception desk loomed large and imposing on the far end of the room, but the presence of framed photographs along its surface softened its effect. The photos showed the smiling faces of families—some with fathers, some without.

Emily had spent many hours wondering if her child would feel cheated by the absence of a daddy. She wondered now if the pictures were meant to reassure.

The receptionist, a pretty blonde with a welcoming smile, checked her in and told her to take a seat.

There were two other women, one obviously pregnant, in the waiting area. They had taken the two available chairs, so Emily moved to the couch. Matthew followed.

All the magazines on the glass tables dealt with mothers and babies. A book entitled *How To Have a Baby Without a Man* sat on top of the stack. If Matthew felt that the place was hurting for reading material, he didn't show it. Gamely, he leaned forward, slipped one of the magazines out of the pile and started reading. Emily chose a recent issue of *Working Mother*, but couldn't concentrate on a single word.

A nurse summoned the two women who had arrived for their appointments before Emily. One by one, three more women arrived. Matthew remained the only man in the waiting area.

"Emily Gardiner?"

From the hallway that led to the examining rooms, a fortyish woman in a white uniform and a periwinkle-blue sweater called Emily's name. She held a flat buff folder in her hands.

My file, Emily realized. *I wonder how much fuller it's going to get before we're through?* She set her magazine on the table and glanced at Matthew. He gave her an encouraging smile.

Innocuous as the exchange was, the nurse picked up on it immediately. She tipped the file in Matthew's direction.

"You can come in with her. Dr. Friedlander is just consulting with Emily today. Exams and lab work will happen tomorrow."

Matthew hesitated, deferring to Emily. "Would you like me to come with you?"

Assuming his hesitation signaled reluctance, Emily smiled gamely and shook her head no. She followed the nurse, whose name tag read Lynn, through the door.

Frowning mightily, Matthew hooked an arm over the back of the couch and crossed an ankle over a knee.

He wanted very much to attend the consultation, but he believed it was Emily's right to ask him, not the nurse's. He was not happy. He was, in fact, a little bit hurt that Emily had answered no.

He noticed the brunette in the chair across from him staring at him over the top of her magazine. Uncomfortable, Matthew rose, under the guise of needing to stretch.

Probably thinks I'm here to donate to the cause.

He glanced down at the copy of *Working Mother* Emily had been reading and wondered how she would fare as a working mother. Would the town accept an unmarried, pregnant librarian leading story hour? The people of True could be thunderously conservative when they wanted to be.

Restless, he moved to stand in front of the glass doors, his hands on his hips, his face lifted to catch the warm rays of sun that were filtered through the glass.

A very pregnant lady approached the doors, and Matthew stepped aside as she entered. Again, his thoughts boomeranged to Emily. He tried to picture her in the advanced stages of pregnancy, but his imagination failed him. In all likelihood, he wouldn't be around to see it, anyway.

In the glass, he saw his own reflection thrown back at him like an accusation. His ragged moustache and beard were gone, but the ache in his soul remained.

His own wife hadn't wanted to have a child with him...but Emily had. He'd come back to True an angry mockery of the young man who had left, and still Emily had asked him to be the father of her child.

To be the father of her child. No, that was not what she had asked. Being a father had little to do with biology. The only involvement she had solicited from him was physical.

Well, he'd be damned if his only contribution to the life of a child—his child—would be biological. And he'd be damned again if he'd let the mother of that child conceive through a sterile procedure in a doctor's office. No, his baby would be made in a bed...or in the living room ... or in the back seat of a car, for all he cared, but not, by God, in a doctor's office!

Spinning on his heel so swiftly that he almost scared the latest arrival right into labor, Matthew strode to the reception desk without a care for the stir he was causing in the waiting area.

"May I help you?" The receptionist attempted a placid smile.

"I need to speak with Emily Gardiner. Right now."

"Emily Gardiner?" Frowning, the young woman reviewed her appointment page. "Umm—"

"She just went in," Matthew told her tersely. "The redhead."

"Oh." Confusion cleared, but the frown remained. Keeping her voice low, the receptionist explained, "She's having a consultation. It shouldn't take more than an hour. There's a coffee shop around the corner—"

"I need to speak to her *now.*"

The door to the reception area opened and the nurse who had escorted Emily away reappeared.

This was the first time in more than a year and a half that Matthew had wanted anything other than solitude. Now he was propelled by an urgent need to keep Emily's plan from progressing any further.

"Caryl Bonspensario," the nurse called, smiling as the woman in yellow rose.

Matthew held out a hand. "Wait." He approached the nurse. "I changed my mind. You asked me if I wanted to sit in on Emily Gardiner's consultation. My answer is yes."

The nurse's brown eyes swept over him, assessing his agitated state and registering her disapproval of his becoming agitated in *her* waiting area.

He was not surprised when she shook her head. "If you will sit down, sir, I will be back in a moment."

"A moment," Matthew repeated. "Is that a medical moment? As in, 'The doctor will be with you in a moment'? Because if it is, I can't wait that long."

The woman in the yellow dress hovered uncertainly, advancing when Nurse Lynn spoke, retreating a step with each word that fell from Matthew's lips.

The nurse's mouth compressed into a line as thin as a zipper.

"Ma'am." Matthew spoke with forced politeness. "All I want to do is talk to Miss Gardiner before she makes any decisions with the doctor. I just remembered something she needs to know."

There was a brief, glaring standoff.

"I will ask Miss Gardiner if she wishes to interrupt her consultation. I will return *in a moment.*"

Executing a military turn, Nurse Lynn marched through the door and down the hall to the doctor's office. She was so immersed in her own indignation that she didn't realize Matthew was behind her until the office had been breached. He brushed past her the moment she opened the door.

The nurse sputtered nonsensically, and Matthew turned to her. "Thank you very much." To the doctor, he said, "Excuse me, I have to speak with Emily."

For the moment, he ignored the shock on Emily's sweet face. He'd come this far, he wasn't about to back off now. Jerking a thumb over his shoulder, he requested, "Would you come into the hall, please?"

Emily stared at him with her mouth open. She glanced at the doctor and saw that he was both surprised and displeased. If Matthew was planning to regale her once again with all the reasons why she shouldn't go through with this, she was going to strangle him.

"Matthew," she said, "I'm sure you can wait until Dr. Friedlander and I are finished." Her voice dripped with the honeyed patience she usually reserved for interruptions during story hour.

Matthew colored a bit, but held his ground. "It can't wait," he insisted, jerking his head sharply toward the door, as if that alone would bring Emily scrambling to her feet.

Astounded by his presumption and greatly bemused by his timing, Emily gritted her teeth and shook her head. She'd come a long way—in emotional investment as well as miles—to make this meeting happen. She had no intention of cutting it short. Neither, however, did she want Matthew to make a scene, so she gestured to the chair beside her.

She turned back to the doctor, hoping she could persuade him that she was a sane person. "Matthew is an old friend from my hometown. He's a little uncomfortable, I think, with the idea of this procedure, but he supports my desire to have a child."

Matthew almost puked. The way she'd emphasized *old friend* and *hometown*, he felt like Goober on "Mayberry R.F.D." And saying that he was "a little uncomfortable" with the idea of the procedure was crap. He wasn't *uncomfortable* with the idea, he *hated* it.

He was, however, uncomfortable with the way Emily was glaring at him. Reluctantly, he seated himself in the chair she indicated.

Over Matthew's head, the doctor nodded at his nurse. "Thank you," he said in dismissal.

Nurse Lynn backed out of the room like a Secret Service agent being forced to leave the president's side.

When the door clicked, Dr. Friedlander cleared his throat. "I believe we were discussing the procedure itself when your friend arrived."

Emily nodded, giving the doctor permission to continue the discussion in Matthew's presence.

"You understand that we may have to repeat the procedure several times before conception occurs," he told her. "We're often successful in four to six cycles. That's four to six months," he clarified for Matthew's benefit.

"Four to six?" Drumming his fingers on the arm of the chair, Matthew pursed his lips. "I could beat that by two months—easy."

"Matthew!" Emily gasped.

Dr. Friedlander closed his patient's file and excused himself as he rose. "I think you two have something to discuss before we continue this any further."

"Oh, no, Dr. Friedlander, really—" Emily rose with the doctor. "Matthew will leave."

The small man glanced at Matthew and shook his head. Emily took a step after him, but Matthew's fingers curled around her upper arm. She looked at him, confusion and resentment burning in her eyes as Dr. Friedlander left the room.

"What is the matter with you!" In a voice as pinched as a creaking hinge, Emily confronted the man whose behavior might have cost her the doctor's approval. "I thought you were here to support me." She pointed to the door. "That doctor thinks we're both crazy. The first consultation helps him decide if I'm a good candidate for the program." She put her hands on her hips, her eyes wide and wounded. "Do you understand? If he has reservations, he doesn't have to help me!"

"I'll help you."

Emily tossed up her hands. "*You'll* help me," she scoffed.

Matthew nodded. "I'll help you."

It seemed to take a very long time for his words to register. When they did, Emily thought she felt her heart skid and come to a stop.

"What do you mean?" she whispered.

Matthew's features adopted a Mount Rushmore-like sternness. "I want to be the father of your child."

"You want to be the donor?"

The stony set of his face broke into a disgusted twist. "Hell, no."

Emily's feelings—her confusion, the trembling hope his words had stirred, the heightened tension of the day—yielded to anger now in one quick, purifying burst.

"Look, Matthew, I don't feel like playing games. Just what exactly *do* you want?"

"I want to father your child," he said, leaning forward until their noses were almost touching, his teeth bared as he growled the rest of his answer, "the old-fashioned way!"

Chapter Nine

She had imagined it a hundred times or more.

Sitting on the banks of Willow Kiss, she had listened to the lulling gurgle of the creek, felt the soft moss between her toes and dreamed of Matthew kneeling beside her, taking her hand and asking her gently, earnestly, perhaps even shyly, to be his wife... forever.

She had never, however, imagined herself sitting on an olive-green bedspread in a budget motel while Matthew implored her to "be practical" and marry him.

The motel room was utilitarian and dark. Everything in it was bolted to the walls, as though the management feared their Formica-topped end tables were irresistible.

Matthew had been pacing from the door to the dresser for the past fifteen minutes, and Emily was beginning to wish that someone would come in and bolt *him* to one spot.

They had said nothing to each other on the drive from the clinic, but now Matthew was delivering a virtual dissertation on the benefits of marriage.

"And thus—" Emily gritted her teeth as he continued "—I believe you will agree that a legal bond can only ease the path for any offspring produced by our union."

He stopped pacing beneath a television set that was bolted high on the wall. He looked directly at Emily for the first time since they'd entered the room.

"So." Tension pursed his lips. "Will you...uh... marry me?"

Emily thought she might cry. There they were, the words she had waited half her life to hear: *Will you...uh...marry me?*

She bit her lip as a sob threatened to escape. Always in her daydreams, Matthew's proposal had made her feel full and buoyant and charmed. Today she felt like a spinster librarian with a limp who was running out of luck and running out of time.

"Why do you want to do this, Matthew?" she asked softly. "You've explained why you think we should get married, but you haven't explained why you want a child."

Matthew's frown dipped so low, it all but blocked his vision. His hands went to the back pockets of his jeans. He chose his words carefully. "I've been thinking about *your* reasons for having a child. They're good ones. And I've been thinking about the child himself. A kid should know who his father is. I want to be there. I want to be involved in the child's life."

"And this marriage," she asked hesitantly, "would it be a permanent one?"

Matthew's face looked like Mount Rushmore again.

"No one can answer that question, Emily. Not for any marriage." His reply came out clipped and hard, and he instantly regretted his tone.

Aware of the tension that was mounting between them, Matthew moved to the bed and sat down beside her. The sweet, clean jasmine scent of her perfume recalled memories of sitting beside her at the creek, and he felt himself relax. He answered her again, more gently, his own eyes questioning.

"How about if we take everything one step at a time and see how it goes. Would you be willing to do that?"

Emily turned her head and gazed out the motel window. Her shoulders lifted in what might have been a shrug or a quiet sigh. Matthew wasn't sure.

"Yes, I would be willing." When she turned back to him, her expression was calm, her tone practical. "But I don't think we should discount the option of artificial insemination."

It took Matthew a moment to register her words. "What are you talking about? What do you think we've been discussing here?"

"Marriage," she stated logically. "Having children. But marriage has little to do with the method we choose to conceive a child."

"The hell it doesn't!" Matthew shot off the bed. He raked a hand through his hair. "Do you honestly mean to tell me you'd rather go through that procedure than make love with me?"

"'Make love.'" Emily repeated the words with infuriating detachment. She remained seated on the bed, her hands folded calmly in her lap, while he resumed his prowl between dresser and door.

"I would prefer it," she said without rancor or challenge, "because we wouldn't really be making love. It would simply be a convenience, and that would make it as clinical as the doctor's procedure."

Her words knifed through him. "It wouldn't be clinical," he ground out, controlling his frustration with an effort.

"How do you know?"

Matthew's jaw clenched. His eyes glittered like diamonds. "Trust me."

Emily's gaze skittered shyly away and her brow puckered in deep concentration. Matthew felt an almost overwhelming need to take her in his arms and *show* her why making love with him would be many things, but definitely not clinical.

I want her, he thought, admitting it to himself plainly for the first time. If Emily decided here and now not to have a child at all, he would still want to make love to her. He hadn't felt such need in a long, long time.

"Emily." His voice was gruff and hoarse.

Her eyes lifted to his. He took a step forward, intending to sit on the bed again, then thought better of it and spoke from where he was. "You say it wouldn't be making love. But we would both feel love for the child we were creating." His mouth tilted ruefully. "There are worse ways to begin a relationship."

Emily's heart weighed heavily in her chest. Yes, she imagined there were indeed worse ways to begin a relationship. Worse things, certainly than being the wife of the only man she had ever loved. If she cared less, it would be easier.

Matthew stood near the dresser with his hands in his pockets, watching her.

Say yes, a voice inside her urged. *You've had only one chance in this lifetime to love a man and now he is asking you to marry him. Say yes.*

But he doesn't love me, her heart cried out.

I need more time, she thought and intended to say so, but when she opened her mouth the word that escaped was "Yes."

Matthew pulled his hands out of his pockets. He sighed audibly. "Thank you."

Emily saw his posture relax and the tension fade from his face. She watched pleasure enter those maddening blue eyes and she thought she saw a flash of relief.

The first stirring of anticipation rose in her breast.

Perhaps Matthew was right. There were worse ways to begin a relationship.

It was the second time Emily had been to one of Matthew Carter's weddings. This second set of nuptials, however, bore little resemblance to the first.

The first time around, the wedding had taken a year to plan. The ceremony had been elaborate.

This time, by mutual agreement the wedding was going to take place in a Salem, Oregon, courthouse. There would be no guests in attendance. Emily had told no one. She was nervous enough without having to answer awkward questions. As far as she knew, Matthew hadn't told anyone, either.

They barely spoke to each other on the ride to Salem and didn't have much more to say once they were in the courthouse.

Marry in haste, repent in leisure.

The old proverb popped into Emily's head, and she wondered what the consequences were if you married in silence.

Outside the door to the judge's chambers, Matthew spoke the first multisyllabic sentence of the morning.

"You look very pretty, Em." His eyes traveled over her. "You make a beautiful bride."

Heat washed in waves up her chest and into her face. Nervously, she glanced down at the single long-stemmed white rose Matthew had given her at the motel this morning.

A bride!

Her dress was sea-foam green, not white. She carried a pocketbook and the rose, rather than a bouquet. Her hair was held off her face with gold barrettes, and there wasn't a veil in sight. But his compliment made her feel exactly the way a bride ought to feel.

Matthew was wearing the first suit she had seen him wear since returning to True. Gray with a barely perceptible blue pinstripe, it emphasized the width of his shoulders and made his blue eyes seem bluer.

"You're a very attractive groom," she returned softly, with a catch in her voice. Truly, he looked as handsome now as he had on his other wedding day ten years ago.

They stood in the hallway of the courthouse, staring at each other, and Emily's smile turned shy. She broke eye contact first and fiddled with the catch on her purse.

I hope this is easier for him than it is for me, she thought magnanimously. *At least one of us should get through this day without an ulcer.*

But Matthew was struggling with his own concerns as he watched his bride-to-be pluck at the clasp of her handbag.

She has no idea what she's getting into, he thought, damning himself for rushing her into this. *She's scared silly already, and she has no idea how difficult marriage can be.*

Swallowing hard, he looked away.

Emily checked her watch.

At five minutes after eleven, a matronly woman in a maroon wool suit opened the judge's door.

"The judge will see you now. Follow me, please."

The woman's voice and eyes were expressionless. Her manner was as severe as the steel-gray hair she wore brushed straight back from her face and twisted into a tight, tiny bun at the back of her head.

Matthew and Emily followed her gloomily, sensing one more blow to romance on their wedding day.

"This is Judge Donnelly," the woman told them without ceremony, motioning for them to take the chairs before the judge's wide mahogany desk.

Judge Donnelly was a plump, white-haired man in his sixties. Everything about him was soft and round—his face was round; his nose was round; what they could see of his stomach behind the grand desk was round. Even his wire-rimmed bifocals were round.

As Matthew and Emily took their seats, Judge Donnelly signed several papers with a flourish.

"Done," he said, placing one of the documents on a pile to his left. "Done," he said again, after signing another page with bold, curling strokes. He finished off the last document, collected all the papers, tapped them on his desk to straighten them and handed them to his assistant, who hovered nearby. "And done."

He smiled at the matronly woman, adjusted his slipping glasses and focused on Matthew and Emily through the thick lenses.

"In the mood to be married, eh?" His booming voice was cheery. His eyes twinkled. He leaned back in his chair, which tilted with him, and placed his clasped hands behind his head. He studied the couple in front of him for several moments. "Known each other long?"

Matthew and Emily exchanged quick glances.

"We've known each other for twenty-two years," Emily answered for both of them.

Matthew's head snapped around to her again as though the information surprised him. Judge Donnelly's eyes popped wide.

"Twenty-two years?" he trumpeted. "Good God, what took you so long?"

He obviously expected to be answered, and Matthew shifted, irritated by the man's probing. He was a judge, after all, not a minister, and they had come to be married, not counseled.

"Our lives moved in different directions." The short reply was all Matthew intended to offer. To hasten the proceedings, he glanced at his watch, but Judge Donnelly refused to be rushed.

"My wife and I met in Bible class when we were kids," he reminisced. "We got married right out of high school. I'd have married her sooner, but she was stubborn. Didn't want the high school graduation to overshadow her wedding. Women are like that." He winked at Emily. "We had a big wedding. I had to wear a tuxedo." He grimaced distastefully. "If I'd been a judge then, I'd have worn my robe."

Leaning as far back as his chair would allow, he narrowed his gaze at the prospective bride. "Sure you wouldn't rather have a fancy ceremony instead of tying the knot in a fat old judge's chambers?"

Emily was startled by the question and its phrasing. "Yes, I'm sure," she assured him. Then she hastened to add, "I don't think you're fat at all...or old."

The judge laughed appreciatively. "You're a kind young woman." He moved his hands from behind his head to the top of his belly. "Kindness is an underrated quality in marriage. Tell me, if you were to receive some unexpected good news, who would you tell first? It's not a trick question, mind you. I'm just asking because the answers are interesting. You'd be surprised by how many people say their mother or father. One young man said he would tell his Yorkshire terrier. He didn't get married that day, as I recall."

Donnelly frowned at the recollection, then looked expectantly at Emily.

She wet her lips and nervously twined her fingers. Perhaps if she kept her answer light and glib...

The truth, of course, was that she would want to tell Matthew. It was the obvious answer and the one the judge expected to hear, anecdotes aside. But for Emily, the truth felt too revealing.

It was that very reluctance that made her answer sound so sincere as she glanced quickly at her intended and said, "Matthew."

Her husband-to-be turned to her, and she ducked her head.

Judge Donnelly looked very pleased. "And you," he said to Matthew, waiting for the prospective groom's full attention before continuing. "Say you received some lousy news, really stinking—what would you do? Would you keep it under your hat, work it out yourself without burdening anyone, or would you dump it all on this lovely young woman?''

Matthew's lips started to curve. ''I'd dump it,'' he said, tipping his head toward her. ''I'd go to Emily.''

Donnelly smiled paternally, nodding in approval. ''Friendship is also an underrated quality in marriage.'' He slapped both palms on his desk. ''Well, let's get started.''

Standing, he lumbered bearlike to a sunny window. The warm rays that sifted through the glass created a golden rectangle in the judge's chambers. He stood within it. ''This is a good spot to get married.''

Matthew and Emily rose to join him.

''Marie will be your witness.'' Judge Donnelly nodded toward the grizzly haired woman who had been standing by silently. ''Son,'' he asked Matthew, ''did you bring a ring?''

As a lawyer, Matthew could not remember a judge ever calling him ''son.'' But he found that here in Donnelly's chambers he had nothing to prove, and the paternal address didn't bother him a bit. He pulled a small box from his pocket, opened it and removed a gold ring. As he slipped the velvet box back inside his jacket, he heard Emily's quick intake of breath.

A ruby flanked by small diamonds sat in the center of a band of interlocking gold links. An inset of platinum provided the setting for the gems and gave the ring a delicate, antique appearance. It was the prettiest ring Emily had ever seen.

The judge cleared his throat and started the ceremony in a clear, robust, resonant voice. ''Join hands, please.''

Matthew's hand was warm; Emily's cold. They gave each other a brief, wavering smile before turning their attention to the man who would unite them in holy wedlock. And they soon realized that he was determined to do it his own unorthodox way.

"Of all our most important relationships," Judge Donnelly began, "marriage is the trickiest. It's the relationship we enter into with the most expectations." He shook his white head and smiled. "Oh, we have plenty ideas of how it *ought* to be. And that's not all bad. But we need a sense of wonder, too. Be eager to make discoveries—about yourselves and about each other, and about marriage itself."

As Donnelly continued, the morning sun grew stronger, and the patch of gold they were standing in brightened.

"There will be times when your life together is so different from your expectations that anger may result, and it's during those times that I ask you to think upon this day. Remember the love and friendship that brought you here. And remember that you came with a great desire to make life easier for each other. There's nothing better than knowing that the person you go to bed with each night will be there in your corner each day."

Emily felt Matthew's fingers tighten on hers and hope beat in her chest.

"Now then..." Judge Donnelly frowned, asked them to state their full names and resumed.

"Do you, Matthew Bradley Carter, promise to love, honor and cherish Emily Isabel Gardiner through good times and bad, through all the most exciting moments of your life and in the most mundane, and do you promise to honor your friendship and your love with truth and fidelity and with a deep and abiding regard for the importance of the bonds you are forging here today?"

Matthew turned to Emily. His eyes were full and serious. "I promise."

"And do you, Emily Isabel Gardiner, promise to esteem the vows you are taking with Matthew Bradley Carter and to let forgiveness, respect and love be your guides in all that concerns your life together?"

Emily nodded slowly, her eyes locked with Matthew's. She whispered the words she had thought she would never say in this context. "I do."

Judge Donnelly beamed at the couple. "Put the ring on her finger, son," he instructed. "And now, by the power vested in me by the bountiful state of Oregon, I pronounce you husband and wife. You may kiss your bride," he told Matthew, adding in a jovial undertone, "but if I were you, I'd wait until you're alone with her. That first kiss as a newlywed should really pack a wallop!"

"You give sage advice, sir. I believe I'll follow it." Matthew grinned at the older man, adding a silent promise to himself and Emily. *I'll try to follow all of it.*

The judge shook Matthew's hand, told Emily she made a beautiful bride, then handed the couple over to Marie, who produced new papers for them to sign. When all signatures were properly executed, the matronly woman moved to her employer's side.

To Matthew and Emily's great surprise, Judge Donnelly wound an arm around his assistant.

"We wish you all the best," he said, concluding his time with them. "I can vouch for the joys of matrimony. When you're with the right person, it just keeps getting better. Would you agree, Mrs. Donnelly?''

Marie looked up at her husband and gave him a broad, protracted wink. "I do, indeed, Your Honor."

Several minutes later, Matthew and Emily walked out into the spring sunshine for the first time as a married couple. The fingers of Emily's right hand wandered to the ring finger of her left.

Newlyweds. The title repeated itself over and over in her mind.

Dazedly Emily headed toward the car. Matthew grasped her by the elbow.

"There's not much point in driving right back." He checked his watch. "It's not even noon. You took the whole day off, didn't you?"

Emily nodded. "I told my aunts I'd be back to close up."

"Hmm. Any chance they could close for you?"

Emily blinked in surprise. "I'd just have to call them. I'm sure they'd be happy to." She started digging through her purse for change.

Matthew stopped her again. "How would they feel about covering for you tomorrow, too? And how would you feel about a honeymoon?"

"A honeymoon?" Breathless, Emily stared at her husband.

"A short one." He shrugged. "It's only midday Friday. If you take tomorrow off, we'll have almost three days."

And three nights.

They hadn't discussed a honeymoon of any duration prior to this, but Emily saw that returning home immediately would make it harder to establish a new relationship, one that was based not on a childhood friendship, but on an adult one. And if that was what Matthew wanted, then so did she.

"We didn't bring anything with us," she reminded him. "No clothes or toothbrushes..."

Matthew's smile was persuasive. "Why don't we wing it? I'm sure we can find what we need."

Nervous anticipation swirled through Emily's body. The woman who planned her meals—not days, not weeks, but *months* in advance—was about to wing her honeymoon!

Extracting a couple of quarters from the bottom of her purse, Mrs. Matthew Carter went back into the courthouse to use the pay phone.

Chapter Ten

"Did you tell your aunts that we're married?"

"Yes."

Emily looked past the wavering flames of the tapers that were the table's only centerpiece. Matthew's hair, trimmed for the wedding, shone like melted butter in the candlelight. He hadn't taken his eyes off her all through dinner.

Reaching for the bottle of chardonnay that was chilling in a wine bucket next to their table, he took the liberty of pouring her a bit more. It had taken her all evening to drink half a glass.

"Were they happy for you?" he asked, pouring more wine for himself and replacing the bottle, still without breaking eye contact. "Or concerned?"

"Happy. I asked them not to tell anyone. I said we'd make the announcement when we got back."

Matthew nodded his approval.

Emily ran a finger up the stem of her goblet and wished that Matthew would find some other point in the room to focus on. They were sitting in a tiny, darkened corner of a candle-lit dining room at the Woodlake Inn. There were two other couples dining at neighboring tables, but Emily felt as if she was alone with Matthew.

They had spent the day driving—and shopping. He had insisted on stopping in Eugene on their drive down to the inn. Pulling out a credit card, he told her to charge anything she wanted.

Having a man other than her father purchase her clothes was a whole new experience for Emily. A highly unsettling experience.

She had assumed he would leave her to her own devices while he made his selections for their impromptu honeymoon. Not so. Matthew had involved himself in her every purchase. It practically paralyzed her in the lingerie department.

Emily had stood immobile and opinionless by the negligees. Obviously anything with the feet in was out of the question. Ditto flannel thicker than a blanket. But to choose something lacy and enticing with Matthew standing by? She had quivered at the intimacy of it all.

Matthew had felt no such qualms. He'd grinned at her hesitation, searching through the racks of negligees himself until he found one he declared would look beautiful on her. It was all clinging cream lace, with tiny peach rosebuds on the bodice.

Even now, as they finished their meal, the nightgown hung like ominous foreshadowing in the closet of their bedroom at the inn.

Matthew took a sip of wine and dropped an inquisitive glance at the dinner she had hardly touched. "Not hungry?"

"Not very."

"Would you like to leave?"

"No!" Thoughts of that nightgown made her answer a bit too emphatically. "I mean, you should finish yours."

He looked down. "I have."

"Do you want some of mine?"

"No."

"Would you like dessert?" She couldn't possibly get into that nightgown. Not yet. They hadn't even kissed as husband and wife. "The people to our left had mousse."

"I don't want dessert." Matthew's eyes wandered lazily over the dress he had chosen for her. "You look wonderful in red."

She blushed under his gaze and self-consciously put a hand to her hair. "I look like a fire engine."

Matthew shook his head. "You look like the fire."

Emily swallowed hard. What was happening? He had never looked at her this way before. And the attraction she had felt most of her life had never seemed quite so...dangerous.

She forced a chummy laugh. "Do you remember the Fourth of July parade that Hurwertzer's Grocery sponsored—when was that, back in '75?—and Gail Springer came dressed as a firecracker with red food coloring all over her face? Now *there* was someone who looked good in red. I remember saying at the time—"

"Emily." On several occasions this evening, she had tried to steer the conversation back to their childhood, and he had interrupted her every time.

Signaling the waiter, Matthew signed the check with his name and their room number, and stood.

The last vestiges of twilight were still clinging to the sky as they walked from the restaurant to their little cabin behind the main building. Tall pines lined the walkway.

Traveling by car for several hours had stiffened Emily's back and hip, making her limp more pronounced. The night, with its beauty and its implications, heightened her awareness of what she perceived as a defect, and she became aware, too, that Matthew was slowing his pace to accommodate her.

When they reached their cabin, she entered first and saw that homey flames were dancing in the fireplace.

"I asked them to light a fire while we were at dinner. Even in spring the nights can be cold up here." Matthew walked past her, loosening his tie. "We have a Jacuzzi. I'm going to fill the tub."

Emily's head swiveled round as he brushed by her on his way to the bathroom. A Jacuzzi? "But we didn't bring bathing suits!"

Matthew halted on the threshold of the bathroom and turned around to look at her quizzically.

Emily clasped her hands in front of her, pressing them tightly. "I'm sorry," she said, wagging her head forlornly. "It's just that I'm a very modest person..." She paused, then amended in pained honesty, "Okay, *sheltered*. I just don't think I would be comfortable. I mean, *maybe*, if we had bathing suits—"

Grasping her by the shoulders, Matthew pulled her toward the bed. Seeing her eyes widen, he swore, shook his head and propelled her sideways to the sofa.

"Sit down."

Emily obeyed, and Matthew sat beside her. Carefully, gently, he took her hands in his.

"Emily, I know you're nervous. We're not going to do anything you're uncomfortable with. And I'm not about to ravish you in a Jacuzzi. I can see that your hip is bothering you, and I just want you to relax in a hot bath—by yourself."

Emily closed her eyes. "I'm sorry," she whispered. "I don't mean to be skittish, but I'm so...so..."

"You're so *married,*" he finished for her. She opened her eyes to his wry smile. "It feels different and new to me, too."

"It does?"

"Yes." His thumbs moved over the tops of her hands. "I'm going to run that bath for you."

True to his word, he prepared the bath—and that was all. Emily got undressed alone and climbed into the tub alone. She was acutely aware of his presence just beyond the bathroom door, but as the hot, foaming water swirled around her hips and back, relaxation came quite naturally.

Through the bursts of water shooting from the powerful jets, she could see her own body, fair and supple against the enamel tub.

She remembered suddenly the times in her late teens and early twenties when she would stand before a mirror as naked as she dared to be—which usually meant she was wearing a bra and panties—and study her own body.

What she had discovered was that she was thin; standing up or lying down, her hipbones were clearly visible. She had determined also that her breasts were too small and that one hip was slightly higher than the other, an effect of the scoliosis. But her legs were long and slender, and her arms were pale and graceful, like a dancer's. How, she had wondered time and again with a wistful curiosity, would a man see her?

After a while, however, she had stopped studying her reflection. She had ceased wondering what a man's opinion of her body would be, because it hadn't seemed likely there was going to be a man to worry about.

Now, after all these years, she cared again. The veil of water was kind—it softened the angles—but she knew that nothing much had changed.

Reaching behind her for the bubble bath she'd spied earlier, Emily poured a healthy capful into the tub. Whipped by the jets, the soap frothed into billowy peaks. Soon she was surrounded by snowy mounds higher than her chin.

Leaning back, the bubbles popping and crackling beneath her head, she tried to clear her mind, but visions of Matthew's eyes and hands teased behind her closed lids.

She stayed in the bath an hour, letting the water lull her when the jets shut off. She might have fallen asleep right where she was, if not for a knock on the bathroom door.

"Emily? How are you doing in there?"

Jerking straight up, Emily inadvertently sloshed bubbles over the side of the tub and onto the floor. "Fine." She turned the single syllable into a song. "I'm fine."

"You forgot your nightgown in the closet. You want me to bring it in to you?"

Her gaze darted around the bathroom. All she saw was a towel and her evening clothes.

"Em, I'm coming in."

"Just a minute!" Hurriedly, Emily considered her options: wrapping herself in the towel and going to the door, or hiding under the bubbles.

"Emily," Matthew called wearily while she hesitated, "I'll close my eyes. Come on, you've been in there over an hour, and I'm getting bored out here."

Out here alone on my wedding night, he elaborated silently, pressing a hand to his tired eyes as he leaned against the bathroom door.

Hell, he hadn't expected her to jump into bed with him. But with his own awareness of her changing rapidly, he found her extreme reluctance to be alone with him on their wedding night a bitter pill to swallow.

"All right. Come in."

Surprised, Matthew straightened away from the door. He glanced at the lacy material in his hands, and to his amazement felt his heart beat harder in response.

Opening the door, he stepped inside the warm bathroom. Immediately his eyes sought the tub and the woman in it. His breath caught and held.

No vision could have pleased him more. What he saw was not a nymph, naked and visible beneath the water, but a fair-skinned, lightly freckled sprite, covered in bubbles. The white froth was stingy, revealing only her shoulders, neck and face, but it was enough to make him hunger to touch her.

"Your hair is full of soap." Striving for a casualness he certainly did not feel, Matthew pointed to the curls that were trailing into the suds. The bulk of the thick red tresses was piled on her head, damp and springy.

"You were supposed to close your eyes," Emily reminded him, but there was no censure behind the words. Her eyes were wide and shy.

Matthew's fingers tightened around the material of her gown as he smiled at her. *Emily, Emily,* he thought, *this is nothing like being kids at the creek.*

He took another step toward her and laid the nightgown on the counter near the sink. A round silver tray with a mirrored bottom held miniature bottles of body lotion, shampoo and conditioner. He reached for the shampoo and quirked a brow at his wife. "Slide over."

"What?"

"Closer to the faucet."

"Wh-why?"

With a provocative smile, Matthew covered the remaining steps to the tub. "I'm going to wash your hair."

"Wash my hair?" Emily's voice squeaked thinly past the tightness in her throat. "In the bathtub?"

"*You'll* be in the bathtub," he confirmed, dropping to one knee beside her. "I'll be right here." He reached a tanned hand toward the topknot of red hair. "Are there pins in this thing?"

"Yes." Her hand flew to her hair, the movement making the bubbles crest. She smiled tremulously. "I was just going to get out."

Matthew trailed his fingers down one of her long, spiral curls. "Emily, *nobody* could see through these bubbles." He inched closer and murmured, "Relax. Hasn't anybody washed your hair before?"

Emily nodded and the first bobby pin was eased slowly away.

"Remember how good it felt?" Matthew asked.

She nodded again, but somehow, the memory of her mother washing her hair in the kitchen sink bore little resemblance to what she felt now.

When the pins were all out, Matthew combed through her hair with his fingers, then reached behind her to turn on the taps.

The high, gracefully arching neck of the brass faucet facilitated the procedure. He wet Emily's hair, then poured on the shampoo. His fingers were gentle and ministering as they delved into the pile of thick, curling locks. With slow, sensuous circles, Matthew massaged Emily's scalp.

Emily had never felt anything so good in her life. She began to relax as he sent shivers of soothing sensation down her neck and into her back. Soon the pattern of his massage became familiar to her; she knew that after the tiny, tingling circles would come the long, luxurious strokes. She was lulled into a dreamy contentment.

Then, just as she thought she was used to his touch, it altered. It shifted subtly, provocatively, and suddenly it wasn't so calming anymore.

By the time Matthew was through, Emily felt his touch all the way down to her toes, though his hands had moved no lower than the base of her neck.

She spoke not a word for fear she might moan.

Twisting her wet hair into a long rope, Matthew carefully looped the cord on top of her head, using the bobby pins to secure it in place.

"There." He dropped a light kiss on the tip of her nose. "Be careful getting out of the tub." Rising,

Matthew reached his arms over his head to stretch out his back. Flashing Emily a grin, he walked to the door, turning to look at her as he reached for the knob. "Remember what Judge Donnelly said about a husband and wife's first kiss?"

It took all of Emily's resources just to summon a nod. Goose bumps shivered on her skin above and below the water.

"That," he informed her, referring to the kiss on her nose, "wasn't it."

When the door closed behind him, Emily scrambled from the tub. She'd used so much bubble bath, she had to shower the suds away.

She availed herself of the lotion on the silvery tray, and then the nightgown went over her head like a ritual symbol of womanhood, changing even the way she felt about her own body. Who could ruminate over a limp or slightly uneven hips when clinging cream lace was highlighting all her best features? And it was lace her *husband* had picked out!

Pulling the pins from her hair, Emily turned to the mirror. Yes, she thought, she was different. As if the mirror were enchanted, it offered up a reflection that was undeniably alluring.

Most importantly, Emily *felt* beautiful. The lace wrapped lovingly around her body, and the hair she had always thought of as too bright and too conspicuous seemed suddenly a glorious thing because her husband had washed it for her.

She wished for perfume, but settled for the clean scent of the moisturizer. Now, more than ever before, she wanted to claim the kind of allure that could captivate a man. And now, for the first time in her life, she thought the possibility might not be not so far-fetched.

She opened the bathroom door without trepidation. The bedroom was draped in moody shadows cast by lamps dimmed low. Matthew was lying on the bed, wearing only his jeans. His arms were folded behind his head and his eyes were focused on the ceiling. When she closed the door behind her, his gaze lowered.

For a moment as he stared, he remained absolutely still. Then slowly he lifted his head, lowered his arms and rose from the bed. On his way to her, he flipped a switch on a CD player and quiet, lilting music filled the room. There was less than a foot between them when he stopped before her.

"Mrs. Carter," he said, his voice low, firm, turning the address into a statement. "May I have this dance?"

He extended his left arm shoulder level. With his right hand he reached for her waist.

Emily could feel her own pulse. In fact, the whole room seemed to be pulsing.

Carefully, she placed her hand in his. As he drew her forward, she summoned the courage to tell him, "I've never danced...I mean, slow-danced before, Matthew. I'm not sure I—"

"You'll love it."

With his hand on her back, he guided their steps. She didn't have to take many—mostly they swayed, but Emily felt as giddy as if she was dancing in a ballroom, instead of a bedroom.

The music wafting from the CD player was dulcet and sweet. "I'll be loving you...always." The lyrics floated to Emily like a benediction.

Matthew pulled her closer. As her breasts pressed lightly against his bare chest, she stiffened and stumbled a step. Their bare feet tangled. He dropped a kiss into her hair, then set her lightly away from him and kept dancing.

Emily knew she was overreacting, but she was confused...so confused! She wanted their relationship to change; she wanted him to make love to her, but not just because they were going to make a baby. She thought he was seducing her here tonight, but her experience was so limited. And suddenly his wanting to make love to her was not enough. She was getting greedy. She wanted more.

As her thoughts tumbled and crashed into one another, her feet grew clumsy. Finally, after several awkward attempts to find synchronization, Matthew stopped and held her away from him.

"Are you tired?"

His eyes held touching concern and, Emily thought, smiling resignation. "I am getting tired, yes," she told him, and then realized, *I have just started my married life with a lie.* "Are *you* tired?" she asked, thinking, *If he says no, then I'll say I'm only a little tired.*

But Matthew didn't answer the question directly. He merely pushed a damp red curl from her forehead and said, "Let's go to bed."

He stepped away from her, leaving her to climb into bed on her own while he pulled new pajamas out of a chest of drawers and retired to the bathroom.

Emily lay in the bed with the covers tucked under her arms and her hands folded on her chest...and then on her stomach, because she thought that would look less provocative...and then on her chest again, because she didn't want him to think that she'd been thinking about what would look provocative and what wouldn't.

She closed her eyes when she heard him turn the knob on the bathroom door. On his way to the bed, he turned off the lamps. The firm mattress barely gave as he got in, but Emily felt the warmth of his body as he moved under the covers. Feeling ridiculous for closing her eyes when she was wide-awake, she let them flutter open again. There was something she had to say to him tonight.

"Matthew?" She whispered into the darkness.

"Hmm?"

Emily felt, rather than saw, him turn his head on the pillow, and though it was much too dark to see clearly, she turned her head, as well.

She thought of Judge Donnelly's words, of Matthew taking her shopping and washing her hair, and of how she had felt when she looked in the mirror and during the first moments of their slow dance.

Emotion filled her voice when she said, "This was the nicest day I've ever had."

The words barely left her lips before his arm snaked around her, pulling her close. Turning her so that her back was snuggled against his chest, he curved his body around her. His thighs came up to rest beneath hers.

"Me, too," he whispered against her ear.

Emily learned two things then as she lay against Matthew, their bodies touching from head to toe: one, her husband did not wear pajama tops; and two, being held in warm, solid arms while you drifted asleep was the most wonderful feeling in the world.

The first full day of their marriage dawned fresh and crisp, as spring mornings in Oregon were apt to be. They ate breakfast in the restaurant that fronted the inn, and then at Matthew's suggestion drove to a stable that was only a few miles from one of the area's several lakes. They went on an hour-long trail ride and Emily experienced another first—riding a horse.

The afternoon was spent out on the lake on a skiff. They bought sandwiches, potato chips and drinks at a convenience store and took the food on board.

If the newlyweds had suffered from a dearth of sexual expression on their wedding night, neither of them was aware of it. The entire day was marked by easy laughter and teasing touches. Like two kids in the early stages of a crush, Matthew and Emily looked for any excuse to make contact. The fact that their attraction was unexpressed merely heightened the sensations.

And, indeed, they *felt* like teenagers again, giddy and excited just to be in each other's company. At one point they held hands and the sensuousness of it was so heady, Emily thought she might swoon. Unbeknownst to her, Matthew felt a bit light-headed himself.

More than once that day, Matthew found himself looking at Emily and thinking, *This is how it should have been, all those years ago.* He knew with a certainty that superseded guilt, superseded even regret, *This is how it was supposed to be—the two of us.*

The sun had begun its westerly descent by the time they returned the boat to the dock. Rather than head immediately back to the inn, they walked together to a grassy knoll to watch the sunset.

Emily was wearing stiff new jeans and a plaid shirt. Her red hair tumbled in waves over her shoulders. Matthew leaned back on his hands and watched her. He smiled as the golden light played upon her and smiled still more when he realized that the colors in the sunset matched the colors in his wife's hair.

A strange sensation settled over him, a feeling he hadn't experienced in so long, he acknowledged it not with the calm acceptance it should have brought, but with a jolt.

Peace.

He felt peace. And an absence of pain. The guilt and the anger that shadowed his days had yielded when he wasn't even looking.

A handsome mallard rose from the shore of the lake for a last flight before twilight.

He was a soaring, gliding silhouette against the russet backdrop, and the vision delighted Emily.

"Oh, isn't that beautiful!" Pleasure glowed on the face she turned toward her husband.

In that instant, Matthew recognized the peace he experienced for what it was: a soul-felt conviction that he was exactly where he was supposed to be, doing exactly what he was supposed to be doing.

And what he wanted to do next, what he felt would be absolutely, unquestionably right, was to make love to his wife.

Determined not to rush her, he reached out to touch her hair. It felt smooth and supple between his fingers. His knuckles brushed her shoulder. Emily's back straightened.

Matthew gritted his teeth and resisted the urge to turn the innocent brush of knuckles into a full and sensual caress.

He commanded himself to proceed slowly.

First, he would rest the back of his hand gently on her nape...just for a moment or two...and then, if she seemed comfortable with that—

He never finished the thought.

Emily turned, and before Matthew could move or think or react, her arms were around his neck and her lips were flush against his.

Unprepared, he fell back against the cool grass. Emily fell with him. Their legs tangled and, protectively, he wrapped his arms around her back, holding her steady on top of him.

Lips. Suddenly, every nerve ending either of them possessed seemed to be located in their lips.

Emily kissed him hard. She felt his surprise and realized that she was kissing him harder than she had intended—not that she'd had a lot of time to think about it. She had felt him lifting her hair, touching her back and—whammo!—she'd lunged at him.

All day long he had teased her, touched her, looked at her when he thought she wasn't looking at him. And all day long, she had tried to concentrate on something other than how wonderful it had felt to sleep in his arms.

The moment she had felt his fingers on her neck, she had lost all control. She had waited a lot of years to kiss and be kissed and she hadn't been willing to wait a minute more.

Now, with her lips pressed to his and her body prone atop him, Emily began to realize that this wasn't precisely the way she had dreamed it would be. What their lips were engaged in wasn't even a kiss, exactly; it was more of a...*smoosh*.

She lifted her head. With a couple of inches of space between them, she opened her eyes. He opened his, as well, and for a moment they stared at each other, immobilized. Then Matthew reached up and cupped the back of her head. His fingers tangled in her hair and with more raw need than gentleness, he pulled her down again.

His arm tightened around her waist. This time it was he who guided the kiss. He urged her lips to part and soon his tongue was engaging hers in a dance not unlike the one they'd shared last night, with Matthew leading and Emily following.

The fingers he spread across her waist began massaging, caressing. Her flesh felt as if it were melting beneath his hand, and the sensations that had been centered on her lips moved down to other parts of her body.

Tightening his hold on her, Matthew rolled very carefully so that Emily was on her back. The pressure of his lips increased.

Already Emily was learning that some kisses told stories and others asked questions. This was a telling kiss: *More to come,* it said. *Count on it.*

Matthew lifted his head to look at her. His eyes were half-closed and sleepy looking. Or maybe it was her eyes that were half-closed; she couldn't tell. Her head was spinning, her heart pounding. He dropped one more kiss on her parted lips, this one quick and light.

"Sun's down."

Emily looked past him to a lavender sky. She nodded.

Glancing up, Matthew judged the lateness of the hour. "Must be eight-thirty. Or later." His voice was filled with regret. "Way past dinnertime."

Emily saw the smile in his eyes. "Way past," she agreed in a whisper.

"Too bad. We may as well go back to the room."

"May as well."

Pushing himself off her, Matthew stood. He reached out to help her up and without a moment's hesitation, Emily put her hand in his.

Chapter Eleven

She was flying.

Emily felt like a bird—soaring, stretching toward a new height, a place she had never flown before. And then gliding effortlessly, her body weightless ... free ... complete.

Never had she imagined that her soul would also feel replete. Never had she imagined that the act of loving would feel like a gift: one given, and one received.

Matthew's last kiss was a claiming kiss: *You're mine,* it told her before it gentled and became a yielding kiss. *I'm yours.*

It was a simple thing to lie silently, side by side, listening to the sound of each other's breathing, feeling the beat of each other's heart. It was harder to speak, to risk the magic of the moment.

Matthew lifted up on an elbow. His body radiated warmth and contentment. With infinite care, he brushed a curl from Emily's forehead, smoothing it onto the pillow.

"You have such beautiful hair," he murmured. "I've always loved it."

Emily smiled. "Liar."

"Liar?" Matthew reared back, his eyes wide with surprise.

"Mmm-hmm. Eighth grade. You wanted to dye my hair brown. With wood stain."

Matthew laughed. "I did not—" He stopped as memory returned. "Oh, yeah, I did." He settled against his bride. "That wasn't a bad color, come to think of it. I stained my baseball bat that color."

Rubbing his bare chest sinuously across hers, Matthew growled next to her mouth, "I loved that baseball bat."

Emily felt her body react immediately. As his nipples brushed across hers, her hands came up to grip his shoulders. She gasped when she felt his tongue circle her ear.

Matthew lifted his head. "Enough of this," he grumbled, raising himself to his elbows and tucking the sheet around his wife. "You're distracting me."

Emily was breathless. "*I'm* distracting *you?*"

He nodded, crooking his forefinger and smoothing it lightly down her temple and cheek. "I have a question for you."

"What?"

He traced the curve of an eyebrow. "Em—" she could feel his deep voice resonate in his chest "—have you ever been in love?"

"Have I—" Caught off guard, her heart beat faster. She took a breath, then smiled. "Yes."

"What happened?"

She placed a hand against his cheek. "He married somebody else."

Matthew shook his head. Turning his face toward her hand, he kissed her palm. "Why didn't you ever make love?"

Emily stared up at him. "Why didn't— What?"

"I wish I'd known before." Lowering his head, he pressed a kiss into the corner of her mouth. He smiled and she felt the smooth surface of his teeth against her closed lips. "I had some idea, of course. You're still so innocent."

"Innocent?" Emily pressed her head back into the pillow, inching away from his kiss.

Matthew's smile broadened. "It's not a bad word, Emily."

"It sounds like one." Pulling the sheet up to her chin, she wondered if she had done something wrong, or if she hadn't done enough. "You think I'm inexperienced," she mumbled into the covers.

"You *are* inexperienced." Tugging the sheet back down, he nibbled on her shoulder. "You're also delicious...very desirable...sexy..."

Goose bumps raced along her arms and down her legs.

He lifted his head again. "Did you say you wanted a boy or a girl?"

Emily looked at him blankly. She hadn't thought about a baby once in two days. She had all but forgotten that having a baby was the reason for their marriage...and the reason for making love.

Matthew pressed his body more closely against her. "The reason I ask," he continued conversationally, "is that I read an article once about choosing the sex of your baby. Apparently it's possible to influence the odds."

"It is?"

"Mmm-hmm. Say you want a girl—" He stopped, cocking his head as though he'd just remembered something. "You did say you want a girl, didn't you?"

"Yes."

"No problem. To influence the odds, Mrs. Carter, you and I will simply have to—" he tugged a corner of the sheet a little lower and kissed the gentle rise of her breast "—switch places."

"S-switch?" Emily struggled to think clearly. Every time he kissed her, her brain came to a standstill.

"Uh-huh." He trailed kisses across her collarbone. "Unless you've decided you want a boy. Then we can stay right where we are."

The kisses traveled up her neck and she felt the tip of his tongue trace the curve of her jaw. She started to smile.

"Well?"

"Well," she repeated, shivering as he worked his way back down to her shoulder, "um . . . what do *you* want?"

"Me?" Matthew settled himself comfortably and framed her face with his hands. "I want one of each."

His grin was the last thing she saw before she wound her arms around his neck and kissed him back.

They settled into a happy pattern over the following week.

During the day, while Matthew renovated Carter House, Emily resumed her work at the library. She quickly discovered that love brought with it a generosity of spirit: overdue books did not bother her; a loose pet hamster in the children's section failed to rattle her; the most tedious tasks no longer seemed boring.

Matthew, too, felt the difference. His every activity assumed new meaning and purpose. A day was not merely *spent* anymore; it was *invested*. Planning the future for Emily and the children they would have consumed his waking moments. He wanted, most especially, to give his wife the best possible life, because she had given him back his joy.

Emily's parents were stunned, but delighted by their daughter's marriage. They came for dinner the week following Matthew and Emily's return, bringing with them a gift from Aunt Ginny and her promise to visit the couple soon. Emily's parents were careful not to tarnish the evening with complaints about the couple's decision to elope, but they insisted on throwing a wedding reception in the not-too-distant future.

On the following evening, Matthew and Emily went together to visit Tom Carter. Tom was as surprised as Emily's parents, but he seemed pleased, and with Emily present as a sympathetic buffer, this meeting proceeded far more smoothly than Matthew and Tom's first visit.

Later that same week, the newlyweds had company again when Emily's aunts dropped by.

"I'm going to give you my aunt Hannah's rocking chair as a wedding gift," Lilly announced over coffee and cookies in Emily's living room. "Every couple should start out with a rocking chair. It's a good omen."

"They don't need that ungainly old thing." Tillie plucked a sugar cookie off a china plate. "I want to give them Mother's cedar chest. It will look wonderful at the foot of your bed, Emily dear. Oh, yours too, of course, Matthew." She giggled into her coffee.

"Tillie, that twittering of yours is unforgivable." Lil shook her head. "We will give them the rocker because Carter House cries out for it. Fisher would love it."

"Fisher would want them to have Mama's cedar chest," Tillie insisted. "It's functional."

"Functional? What do you think you're sitting on—thin air?"

Emily looked at her husband in appeal. *Help,* she mouthed as the twins argued over the better gift.

The phone rang and Emily started up from the couch, but Matthew beat her to the punch. "I'll get it," he whispered, grinning. "You stay here and talk to your aunts."

"Snake," she hissed, returning the grin before he headed to the extension in the kitchen.

Sighing happily, Emily set about soothing her aunts' ruffled feelings.

"They would both make wonderful gifts," she said sincerely, "but maybe we should hold off awhile. I don't know if we're even going to be living in Carter House."

"Not live there?" Tillie looked at her niece in alarm. "Where will you live?"

"Here, for now. We haven't really discussed it. I'm not sure what Matthew's plans are for the house."

"Oh." Tillie shared a glance with her sister, who was frowning mightily. "He wouldn't sell it to strangers, would he?"

Both women hung on their niece's reply, and Emily realized with regret that she didn't have an answer to give them. "How about if I tell you as soon as I know?"

Tillie nodded. With her blue-white hair and her short, quick head movements, she looked like a bird. "I think it would be heavenly to live in that old house. To fill it with people and light it up at night." Her eyes and voice held longing, and Lil, too, looked wistful.

Emily was beginning to feel a bit dreamy herself, so she changed the subject, asking her aunts what they thought of puffed pastry with spinach soufflé as an appetizer for the reception.

Matthew returned to the living room thirty minutes later. Emily smiled up at him, but Matthew was so distracted he barely noticed her.

"I apologize, ladies." His glance included his wife. "I left a few things unfinished at the house today. I need to get back to it."

"It's almost eight o'clock," Emily protested lightly.

He nodded. "Don't wait up for me. I may be late."

No one said a word until Matthew closed the door behind him. Then Tillie started discussing a new bundt cake recipe using lime gelatin. Lil picked up her end of the conversation and, in an effort to spare their niece embarrassment, the two women chattered away. It became clear before long, however, that Emily was too preoccupied to appreciate the gesture. Finally, Tillie moved to the sofa to sit by her niece.

"You mustn't mind him, Emily. Men can be so moody at times." She smiled fondly. "But he cares for you deeply, I can tell."

Lil added her nodding agreement, and Tillie reached for Emily's hand. "I can't tell you how happy we are for you. Lilly and I—we know what it's like to live alone. We have each other, of course, and we're grateful to your parents for taking us in with them. But to have a home of one's own, a husband and a chance for a family! Oh, my!"

She pressed a delicate hand to her chest. "You deserve every bit of your good fortune."

"Every bit of it," Lil echoed.

Tillie's soft blue eyes glistened. "I hope you'll understand, dear, when I tell you that we're living a little of the dream right along with you."

"Oh, Aunt Tillie." Emily drew the woman close for a hug, then reached a hand out to Lil. "I love you," she told them, her own eyes growing moist. *I just hope there's enough fantasy to go around.*

Matthew walked through the door shortly after the digital clock clicked to midnight. Emily lay in bed, listening to him move about the house, turning off the lights on his way to the bedroom.

The floor creaked as he approached the bed, and she heard him halt abruptly.

"It's all right. I'm awake."

Reaching up to snap on the bedside lamp, Emily blinked at the sudden glare. When her eyes were able to focus, she noted her husband's appearance with surprise. His shirt was only half-buttoned and his hair was wet.

"Where have you been?"

"Working on the house." Matthew stripped off his shirt and unbuckled his belt. "I took a shower there so I wouldn't wake you. Why are you up?"

"I was worried about you. You left so suddenly." Sitting up, Emily gathered the covers around her waist, smoothing the blanket neatly over her legs. "That must have been quite a phone call." She smiled. "I mean, it certainly had a strong effect on you."

Matthew was bending over a dresser drawer. He went still and tense, and Emily immediately regretted her clumsy probing. Her hands flew to her cheeks.

"Oh, I'm sorry!" she blurted, shaking her head. "All night I've been telling myself not to say anything. Your phone calls are your business." She buried her face in her hands.

"Don't, Emily!"

Matthew's voice snapped like a whip. He was across the room in a flash, grabbing her wrists, pulling her hands from her face. "Don't apologize because I was rude."

Emily looked at her husband's taut, troubled features. "I'm so confused," she whispered.

"About what, Em?"

She shrugged, looking as miserable as she felt. "How to be a wife."

Gathering her in his arms, Matthew held her tightly. He smoothed a hand over her hair, then pulled back to look at her. "You haven't heard me complaining, have you?"

They sat quietly for a few moments, Emily leaning against the headboard and Matthew sitting on the side of the bed with his feet on the floor.

"The phone call was from my law firm," he said finally. "They think it's time I made a decision about going back."

"Going back?" Emily repeated, feeling dazed.

Or perhaps, she realized dully, the problem was that she had been in a daze ever since the wedding. The past week had been her fantasy come true. None of the whys or wherefores of their marriage had seemed important these last days. Now she became acutely aware that although they had taken vows of "forever," what they had really meant was "for now."

She strove for a level, unemotional tone. "What do you want to do?"

Matthew turned to her. His eyes were so filled with confusion, Emily was torn between fear and the overwhelming desire to comfort him in whatever way she could.

She raised a hand to his forehead, gently combing the strands of wet hair that fell onto his brow. Matthew captured her hand in his.

"You know what I *don't* want to do? I don't want to talk about it tonight." He looked at her apologetically. "Is that all right?"

I'm making discoveries about marriage already, Emily realized, thinking of Judge Donnelly's words. Tonight her needs conflicted with her husband's. She needed to talk; he needed time. Tonight, his needs would come first.

Reaching for him, she slid over on the bed. Tugging Matthew down with her, she wrapped herself around his big body, determined that tonight *he* would know the joy of being nestled in arms that were safe and loving and warm.

Chapter Twelve

"Lemon chiffon." Matthew stepped back, nodding as he studied the section of wall he had just painted. "I like it."

Kneeling on a tarpaulin that covered the hardwood floor, he tipped a can of the paint labeled Lemon Chiffon over a long pan. The pale yellow liquid poured like heavy cream.

He liked the color because it reminded him of Emily—and because he thought *she* would like it. This morning, he had finished replacing the cornices in the living and dining rooms because he knew she liked cornices. Tomorrow he would start the repairs to the front porch because his wife loved a wraparound porch.

Whatever he did to the house from now on—whatever he did in his *life* from now on—would be done with Emily in mind. It had to be that way, because he loved her.

He knelt on the floor, remembering the sweetness of her embrace last night. He wanted a daughter, he decided. He wanted to give the world another woman like his wife. There would be a man someday who would thank him for it.

"My son-in-law," he said aloud and grinned.

As he pushed the roller through the paint, his smile faded. No man would be good enough for this little girl. He was pretty damn certain he wasn't good enough for Emily.

Standing, Matthew rolled paint over the next section of wall.

The phone call he had received from his law firm last night confused the hell out of him. "Fish or cut bait" had been the gist of the conversation. They wanted him back, and they wanted him back now.

Before Emily, there would have been no dilemma: he'd have cut bait.

He didn't care about the money anymore, and he didn't care about the prestige. Not for himself. But for Emily?

He dipped the roller in the pan and released a ragged sigh. He wanted the best of everything for her—and for their children. When he told Emily he loved her and that he wanted to spend the rest of his life with her, he wanted to offer her more than a struggling craftsman for a husband.

His confrontation with his father haunted him all of last night and most of today: *"You'll have a family again someday. You've never had to struggle...."*

Damned if he wasn't repeating the argument in his own head—and this time he was playing both sides himself.

Money was not the glue that held a family together. He knew that. But it killed him to think that the career he wanted would rob the woman he loved of the comforts she deserved.

"Knock-knock." The screen door creaked open and a voice called from the entry. "Are we disturbing you?"

Tillie and Lilly Gardiner stepped lightly into the living room. Matthew set the roller on the edge of the pan and wiped his hands on a rag.

"You're out and about early this morning." He smiled at his in-laws.

The sisters exchanged a glance. "We have quite a bit to do today," Tillie said. "So we thought we'd get a jump on it."

"Early bird gets the worm." Lil nodded. She moved farther into the room, rubber-soled shoes squeaking across the wood floor. "You've done quite a bit of work to the place already. I like that paint."

"So do I." Tillie sniffed several times. "The smell of paint always makes me a little light-headed."

"Would you like to go out to the porch?" Matthew offered.

"Oh, no," Tillie giggled. "I like it."

"We realize that we are interrupting your work." Lil faced him, her back straight, her neck stiff, her head high. She held her hands tightly at stomach level, a navy blue purse dangling off one wrist. "I want to assure you that we are here for a purpose."

Matthew nodded. The twins were in a strange mood, shooting each other mysterious, conspiratorial glances. "What can I do for you?"

Lil squared her shoulders manfully. "We have it on good authority that you may sell Carter House upon completion of the renovations."

Matthew frowned. "You talked to Emily about it?"

"To...a reliable source," Lil said, drawing her words out solemnly. "We would like to know, if you don't mind, whether this is true."

"We're asking for a reason," Tillie interjected, smiling to soften the request.

"I may sell it, yes."

"Matthew..." Lilly took another step toward her nephew-in-law. Tillie inched in closer, as well. "We have a proposition for you...."

At eight o'clock that evening, Emily sat at her dining table—alone. Her husband hadn't come home and he hadn't called. His dinner had gone cold an hour ago.

The best-laid plans... Emily thought with a sigh, blowing out the candles she'd picked up on her way home from work. So much for her romantic dinner. And so much for her hope that Matthew would rush home—if not eager, then at least willing to discuss his plans for the future.

Carrying the dishes to the sink, Emily tried to decide what she should do.

"If this were a real marriage, I'd *demand* that he talk to me tonight." She scraped cold scalloped potatoes into the garbage disposal. "I'd demand an apology, too. The least he could have done was call me so I wouldn't worry."

Hearing her mistress's voice, Jo jumped onto the sink with a little grunt of hello. Sadly, Emily ruffled the cat's fur. "Looks like it's just you and me tonight, kid."

Jo meowed once and jumped down.

"Traitor," Emily mumbled as the little cat trotted out of the room. *Not that I blame you. This place seems twice as lonely now when he isn't here.*

Running the water in the sink, Emily knew she would have a frustrating evening ahead as she waited for Matthew to come home.

"And feeling helpless all the while," she grumbled resentfully. Balling her hands into fists, she thumped the sink. "This is *my* marriage, too!"

Last night she made a discovery about relationships. Tonight, she was making one about herself: she didn't want a sham marriage. The past week had been a fantasy come to life, but she no longer wanted a fantasy. She wanted the real thing—for better, for worse; in sickness and in health; for richer, for poorer... forever.

All or nothing.

"Matthew Carter," Emily whispered into the silence of the cottage, "it's time you and I had our first fight."

The front door to Carter House was open and the house was ablaze with lights.

Emily opened the screen and let herself in, pausing only slightly as the paint fumes assailed her. The furniture was pushed to the center of the room and covered with tarpaulin. There was no sign of Matthew downstairs, so Emily headed to the second story. Halfway up the stairs, she heard singing.

"Ohhh, McCarthy were dead and McKinney didn't know it and McKinney were dead and McCarthy didn't know it and they both lay dead in the very same bed and neither knew that the other were dead!''

Emily entered the master bedroom just as Matthew was embarking on another chorus. He punctuated the "Ohhh" with a long, broad sweep of the paint roller.

"Hello." She raised her voice to be heard above the song.

Matthew spun around. "Em!" A happy grin spread across his face. He laid the roller in a pan and started toward her. "Hiya, dollface. I hope you want to get something to eat, 'cause I'm a hungry painter!''

"'Hiya, dollface'?" Emily flung a hand up, palm out. It connected with Matthew's chest.

She glared at him, undisguised shock scrawled across her features. He was not the picture of moody torment she had envisioned. He had not been holed up here, agonizing over the decision to return to Boston or not, wondering how it would affect her. At least when she had pictured him tormented, she had felt some charity. But to come here and find this... this... *cheerful* person!

She dropped her hand. "Have you been here all night?"

Matthew frowned. "Sure. Where else would I be?"

"And you've been here just... just painting all this time?"

"Emily—" Matthew reached for her arm "—I wanted to—"

She backed away from his grasp. "Matthew Carter, I think your insensitivity today has been nothing short of appalling!''

Matthew's frown deepened. "Em—"

She held up a warning finger. "Don't 'Em' me. I came here because I have something to say to you, and, by golly, I'm going to say it!"

She lifted her chin and met his gaze as calmly as she could. "I was very concerned last night when you told me about the phone call. I didn't pursue it because I didn't want to pressure you, but that doesn't mean I expected to drop the issue altogether!"

She puffed herself up like a bantam hen. "Your future directly affects me now, and I think I should have some say in it. You left this morning before I got up and then you didn't even come home for dinner! I don't think that's fair at all."

Matthew was looking at her as though he had never seen her before. Emily wasn't sure if that was good or bad, but she forged ahead.

"I want a real marriage, Matthew, the kind Judge Donnelly talked about. Remember? He asked us whom we would go to with good news or bad. We said each other." She spread her hands in earnest appeal. "So if we meant that then we have to talk this out together. You can't just hole up in here and decide on your own whether you're going back to Boston or not. That leaves me floundering around not knowing what's going on or how my future will be affected by you. Or if I even have a future with you."

"*If* you have one with me?" Matthew interrupted, before she could take another breath. "What does that mean?" He reached for her, putting his hands on her shoulders. "Emily, what do you think I've been doing all day? I'm trying to decide what would be best for us. Not just me—*us*."

"Us," Emily repeated softly. She shook her head, a profound sense of relief spreading through her as she absorbed his words. "Then you're not planning to go back to Boston on your own?"

"For God's sake," he exclaimed, his frown deepening as his surprise heightened. "Of course not!"

Emily started to smile, but her husband's next words made the smile slip slowly from her face.

"I've been trying to decide if we should *both* go back to Boston." His hands tightened on her shoulders. "I'm reasonably certain it's the right move. It'll be a big change for you at first, so we can make the move slowly, if you want to. I'll need to go back fairly soon, but you could—"

"I could strangle you," Emily interrupted quietly, shrugging away from his hands, *"that's* what I could do."

Shoving her hands into her skirt pockets, she looked into his confused blue eyes and took a deep breath. "I want a *real* marriage," she repeated. "The kind where husbands and wives decide things together. And I don't think I can settle for less. You said we should take it a step at a time," she reminded him, wrinkling her brow. "You said all marriage is hard and that wait and see what happens. Well, I don't want to wait and see. I don't care how hard marriage is, and I don't care about the statistics. I want to make a commitment to *this* marriage. I'm willing to work at making it work."

She rushed on when Matthew looked like he was going to speak. She knew she had to get through this while her courage held. "I don't want to stay married in order to have a baby, either. I can do that alone. I want to stay married because . . . I love you!"

When she finished, there was silence. Total silence. The kind of silence that begged for someone to fill it.

"Aren't you going to say anything?" Emily whispered.

Slowly, Matthew nodded. "Yes, I have something to say." He took a step closer, reaching for Emily's hands, holding them tightly as he murmured, "Emily Gardiner Carter, will you marry me?"

Emily felt her eyes fill with tears even as her heart filled with hope. "Marry you?" Her voice was barely a whisper.

He brought her hands to his lips, nodding again. "No reservations, no holding back. I don't think I could settle for anything less than a real marriage, either." He smiled slightly and shrugged. "As for the statistics, how bad can they be for best friends who fall in love?"

"Oh, Matthew." Emily walked into his arms. She rested her forehead on his chest and curled her fingers into his paint-stained shirt.

Matthew hugged her close. "Emily," he murmured into her hair, "look at me a minute." He put a finger under her chin and tipped her head up. "I'm sorry I hurt you today. I never meant to exclude you from a decision. All I've been able to think about since the firm called me is what would be best for you...for us."

"But how could you possibly know unless you asked?" Emily admonished softly.

He shook his head. "I love you, Em. I knew it the day we got married." Letting go of her chin, he studied her face and grinned. "You looked so nervous. You should have seen your face when Judge Donnelly told me to make sure that our first kiss packed a wallop." His grin exploded into a laugh. "You turned bright red."

She proved his words by blushing again. "Well, you should have seen *your* face. You looked pretty nervous yourself that day, mister."

"Me?" Matthew shook his head, flashing a broad smile. "Nah." Lowering his head, he swept his wife into a kiss that nearly made her blush again.

When they surfaced, Matthew held Emily slightly away from him.

"All right, Mrs. Carter. Here's your choice. Would you like to be the wife of a corporate attorney who can—and will gladly—give you anything your heart desires? Or the wife of a wood carver whose career is guaranteed to be all uphill for the next few years?"

Emily wound her arms around her husband's neck. "The attorney's not too smart if he hasn't figured out that *he's* what my heart desires. My money's on the wood carver."

Matthew stopped her when she would have kissed him. The hope in his eyes made her smile. "Em, are you sure? In Boston we'd have—"

Emily put two fingers to his lips. "A frustrated lawyer and a homesick librarian. We'll have all we'll ever need right here." She dropped her fingers and her smile turned shy. "I loved you when you were whittling sticks by the creek, you know."

Matthew gazed at his wife in wonder. "Is that true?"

She barely had a chance to nod before he crushed her to his chest, claiming the kiss he'd halted a moment ago. They lingered in each other's arms.

Emily sighed dreamily. "I'm going to love raising a family with you in this big old house."

Matthew stiffened. "Oh-oh."

"Oh-oh?" Emily glanced up. "Oh-oh what?"

"Oh-oh, we'll have to ask the new managers."

"What do you mean?"

"I mean there's something else I need to discuss with you." He clasped his hands against her back and leaned slightly away from her. "I always intended to ask whether you wanted to move to Boston or stay here. But I wanted to hedge my bets a little. That's what I've been doing here today."

"Meaning?" Emily prodded.

"Welcome to Carter House Bed-and-Breakfast Inn, Mrs. Carter, where your husband hopes to offer you a reasonable living while he carves clocks and tables... and cradles."

"A bed-and-breakfast inn." Emily felt dazed.

Matthew nodded. "This is a good area for it. And we'll need the income if you're going to turn down proposals from lawyers."

She smiled. "Who are the new managers?"

"The Misses Tillie and Lillian Gardiner.

"They're very capable. You'll like them." He kissed her forehead and the tip of her nose. "Nothing's settled yet. It's up to you, Em. If you agree, then your aunts would like to handle the day-to-day running of the place."

"A bed and breakfast inn," Emily mused, her voice breathy with wonder.

"We don't have to decide now." Matthew was quick to reassure her, and Emily smiled because she saw the endearing eagerness in his words.

"Hmm..." Feigning uncertainty, she pursed her lips and considered the possibilities aloud. "The house would be filled with people in the summer. I'd have a happy, fulfilled husband and two delirious aunts." She shrugged. "I guess I could live with that." Her eyes widened. "We'll have to sell the cottage."

"Uh, actually, I thought we'd stay in the cottage awhile, at least until we have kids." Matthew leered at her meaningfully. "It's more private."

"I see." She heaved a hearty sigh. "Well, at least I'm married to a man who know what he wants. Eventually."

Matthew saw the teasing glint in her eyes and relaxed into a pleased grin. With tantalizing slowness, he lowered his head. "I know what I want right now."

His kiss was lazily seductive. When it ended, Emily leaned against him for support.

"How did you come up with the idea of asking my aunts?" she murmured, loving the feel of his warm hands caressing her back.

"Your aunts came to me, love."

Call me that again, she thought. "They did?"

"Mmm-hmm. They couldn't stand the thought of Fisher's house going to strangers."

Emily lifted her head. "They certainly are attached to this place."

Matthew braced his legs wider so she could snuggle more fully against him. "Not just to the place," he corrected. "Did you know your aunts were in love once?"

"Aunt Tillie told me, but I can't believe she mentioned it to— Oh, my gosh." Her lips parted in amazed realization. "Fisher!"

"Right."

"Both of them?"

"Yep." He smiled, sharing her incredulity. He could hardly believe that his quiet, eccentric uncle had enjoyed not one but two ladies swooning over him.

"Why didn't they ever do anything about it?" Emily exclaimed. "They lived in the same town all their lives!"

"I think that was the reason, sweetheart." Matthew reluctantly released his hold when Emily pulled away from him. "Can you imagine Fisher choosing one of them?"

"They didn't want to hurt each other." She sat on the tarp-covered bed. "I bet they never stopped loving him."

Matthew sat down beside her. When she shook her head, he asked, "What are you thinking?"

Emily turned toward him, her eyes filled with all the tenderness and all the love in her heart. "I was thinking that I'm glad I'm an only child. I could never be selfless enough to let you get away. Not if I knew you loved me, too."

"And I do." Tender and low, Matthew's voice wrapped her in a love that was well worth the wait. "With all my heart, my love, I do."

Epilogue

It was a beautiful day for a wedding.

Emily Gardiner Carter paused on the threshold of a runner that traveled the length of the yard behind Carter House. Ernest Gardiner stood to her right, fidgeting nervously as he prepared to escort his daughter down the aisle. Emily squeezed his arm.

In contrast to her father, she felt no anxiety at all— just a tingling excitement because she was about to renew her wedding vows to the man who had made this the best year of her life.

Matthew stood beaming at the opposite end of the aisle. Their eyes met, and he winked. Emily winked back, a silent message that she was holding up just fine.

As the familiar strains of the Wedding March cued her walk down the aisle, Emily took her first eager steps toward her groom. She moved with the odd step-hitch-step gait she'd had since she was a child, but no one among the wedding guests took any notice. Neither did Emily.

To her left, her mother and Aunt Ginny snapped pictures. To her right, her father-in-law smiled. The past year had brought a measure of healing to Tom Carter and his son, and though their reconciliation was far from complete, Emily wasn't worried. Love, she had discovered, could yield miracles.

Two of those miracles were in the front row.

Bradley James Carter and Meredith Rose Carter snuggled in the arms of their great-great-aunts. Tillie and Lillian glowed as they held the sleeping babies. Emily felt a wondrous sense of peace at the sight of two generations of twins—her children and her aunts.

When she and her father neared the end of the aisle, Matthew grinned, and Emily's heart thumped more quickly. He was still the handsomest groom she had ever seen, the only groom she had ever wanted. He was her lover, her mate, her very best friend.

Her life was full because of him, and she realized that—as good as the past year had been—the best was yet to come.

Stepping close to her husband's side, Emily put her hand in his and returned his joyous grin. She felt like the bride in a fairy tale as she gazed at him.

Matthew Bradley Carter, she vowed, *I'll love you till the day I die.*

* * * * *

JINGLE BELLS, WEDDING BELLS:
Silhouette's Christmas Collection for 1994

Christmas Wish List

*To beat the crowds at the malls and get the perfect present for *everyone,* even that snoopy Mrs. Smith next door!

*To get through the holiday parties without running my panty hose.

*To bake cookies, decorate the house and serve the perfect Christmas dinner—just like the women in all those magazines.

*To sit down, curl up and read my Silhouette Christmas stories!

Join *New York Times* bestselling author Nora Roberts, along with popular writers Barbara Boswell, Myrna Temte and Elizabeth August, as we celebrate the joys of Christmas—and the magic of marriage—with

$\mathcal{J}$INGLE
BELLS,
$\mathcal{W}$EDDING
BELLS

Silhouette's Christmas Collection for 1994.

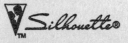

JBWB

Dark secrets, dangerous desire...

Lovers DARK AND DANGEROUS

Three spine-tingling tales from the dark side
of love.

This October, enter the world of shadowy
romance as Silhouette presents the third in their
annual tradition of thrilling love stories and
chilling story lines. Written by three of
Silhouette's top names:

LINDSAY McKENNA
LEE KARR
RACHEL LEE

Haunting a store near you this October.

Only from

Silhouette®

...where passion lives.

MIRA™

The brightest star in women's fiction!

This October, reach for the stars and watch all your dreams come true with **MIRA BOOKS**.

HEATHER GRAHAM POZZESSERE
Slow Burn in October
An enthralling tale of murder and passion set against the dark and glittering world of Miami.

SANDRA BROWN
The Devil's Own in November
She made a deal with the devil...but she didn't bargain on losing her heart.

BARBARA BRETTON
Tomorrow & Always in November
Unlikely lovers from very different worlds... They had to cross time to find one another.

PENNY JORDAN
For Better For Worse in December
Three couples, three dreams—can they rekindle the love and passion that first brought them together?

The sky has no limit with **MIRA BOOKS**.

HE'S MORE THAN A MAN,
HE'S ONE OF OUR

DAD ON THE JOB
Linda Varner

Single dad Ethan Cooper didn't have time for women. But he needed Nicole Winter's business to get his new company going. Then he saw his latest client play mother to his two kids and he wanted her for so much more....

Dad on the Job is the first book in Linda Varner's **MR. RIGHT, INC.**, a heartwarming new series about three hardworking bachelors in the building trade who find love at first sight—construction site, that is! Beginning in October.

Fall in love with our Fabulous Fathers!

WILD RIVER

Maddening men...winsome women...and the untamed land
they live in—all add up to love!

A RIVER TO CROSS (SE #910)
Laurie Paige

Sheriff Shane Macklin knew there was more to "town outsider"
Tina Henderson than met the eye. What he saw was a generous
and selfless woman whose true colors held the promise of love....

Don't miss the latest Rogue River tale, A RIVER TO CROSS, available
in September from Silhouette Special Edition!

SEWR-5

BABY'S CHOICE

Join Marie Ferrarella—and not one, but two, beautiful babies—as her "Baby's Choice" series concludes in October with *BABY TIMES TWO* (SR #1037)

She hadn't thought about Chase Randolph in ages, yet now Gina Delmonico couldn't get her ex-husband out of her mind. Then fate intervened, forcing them together again. Chase, too, seemed to remember their all-too-brief marriage—especially the honeymoon. And before long, these predestined parents discovered the happiness—and the family—that had always been meant to be.

It's "Baby's Choice" when angelic babies-in-waiting select their own delivery dates, only in

Silhouette ROMANCE™

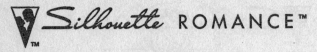

Silhouette ROMANCE™

presents

TIMELY MATRIMONY
by
Kasey Michaels

Suzi Harper found Harry Wilde on a storm-swept beach. But this handsome time traveler from the nineteenth century needed more than a rescuer—he needed a bride to help him survive the modern world. Suzi may have been a willing wife, but could a man from the past be a husband for all time?

Look for *Timely Matrimony* in September,
featured in our month of

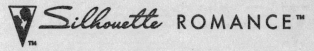

$\blacktriangledown$ *Silhouette* ROMANCE™

**First comes marriage.... Will love follow?
Find out this September when Silhouette Romance
presents**

Hasty Weddings

Join six couples who marry for convenient reasons, and still find happily-ever-afters. Look for these wonderful books by some of your favorite authors:

#1030 *Timely Matrimony* by Kasey Michaels
#1031 *McCullough's Bride* by Anne Peters
#1032 *One of a Kind Marriage* by Cathie Linz
#1033 *Oh, Baby!* by Lauryn Chandler
#1034 *Temporary Groom* by Jayne Addison
#1035 *Wife in Name Only* by Carolyn Zane